The Rise

By

Greg S. Reid

The Rise by Greg S. Reid
Copyright © 2012 by Greg S. Reid

Sherpa Press
2510 Warren Ave Suite 3898
Cheyenne, WY 82001
www.sherpapress.com

ISBN 978-0-9829850-9-0
eISBN: 978-0-9829850-8-3
Library of Congress Cataloging Data

All rights reserved under International Copyright Law. Contents and/or cover may not be reproduced in whole or in part in any form without the express written consent from the publisher.

The Rise

By

Greg S. Reid

Appreciation

In addition to Summer Felix, special thanks and acknowledgement go out to all the leaders and dreamers who make this world a better place. They are always examples of service!

Introduction

Over the centuries, lessons have best been absorbed through parables and stories passed along from one generation to the next. This book continues that tradition with a modern-day tale that reinforces the strategies for personal and business success that have stood the test of time.

Throughout these pages, you will be reminded of age-old wisdoms, which may rekindle the entrepreneurial spirit that made this nation so great and that lies within you, ready to be shared with the world.

Enjoy and whatever you do…. Keep smiling!

Contents

Chapter 1	Remembering Why	11
Chapter 2	Driving Intervention	27
Chapter 3	The Iceberg Melts	35
Chapter 4	Leap and It Will Arrive	41
Chapter 5	Bouncy Ball	45
Chapter 6	Play Up Your Limitations	51
Chapter 7	To Do List	57
Chapter 8	Power of Three	63
Chapter 9	To Move Up, You've Got To Move Down	69
Chapter 10	Look Around	75
Chapter 11	A Lesson in the Way	79
Chapter 12	The Best Shots	85
Chapter 13	Constant Reminders	89
Chapter 14	Remember Who You Are	93
Chapter 15	You're Different Now	97

Chapter 16	Body Armor	101
Chapter 17	Behind the Stage	105
Chapter 18	The Pyramid	109
Chapter 19	What Keeps You Up At Night?	113
Chapter 20	Frame by Frame	115
Chapter 21	The Pay Off	121
Chapter 22	Looking Ahead	127
Chapter 23	Psychology of Referrals Flip the Stats	133
Chapter 24	Give Away Too Much	139
Chapter 25	Authentication Request	141
Chapter 26	Push Don't Pull	145
Chapter 27	The Last Interview	149
Chapter 28	Touching Torches	151
Chapter 29	The Rise	153
Co-Author Biographies		157

Chapter 1

REMEMBERING WHY

Jim MacDonald pushed away the wrinkled sheets and sat up in his black underwear and navy socks. He rubbed his face and walked over to the blaring alarm clock located at the opposite end of the room. The ability to press snooze while still lying in bed would make him late for work. Getting up and enduring the sharp pain of fatigue was the only assurance that he made it to his desk on time each morning.

The towel hanging on the chair in his bedroom still felt damp from his shower the night before. He needed another hot shower; something to help the transition from sleep to boredom. His mind was accustomed to this routine. His only excitement as of late was Friday afternoons. He could leave work early those days, head home, watch his favorite movies and sleep in for two more days. Monday kept coming and with each one, there was less enthusiasm for the week ahead.

He waited for the water to heat up. Above his apartment, he could hear Julia walking around with her son. Her heels were clacking on the wood floor. Following her were tiny thumps going at a faster pace. He could hear her mothering voice speak to him as they rushed to leave. As soon as the door slammed he felt sad. Every morning, the slam of Julia's door represented the beginning of a new day, but not in the refreshing way one would think. It was just another day. Julia and Nathan left the apartment and would return around the same time as Jim. She would be in her work clothes; seemingly happy and Nathan would be covered in dirt smudges and something sticky on his hands. Jim and Julia would greet each other and ask how their respective days were. After the usual 'fine' responses, they went into their apartments. Jim would listen to them run around and play. He could smell her cooking while Nathan watched cartoons and he could always tell when it was bedtime.

The door slammed. He clenched his eyes and completed his shower. It's the sign he has approximately 15 minutes to pop bread in the toaster, throw on clothes and make himself presentable for work.

His journalism goals somehow landed him the complacent job as editor for a local examiner periodical in Philadelphia. What started as a stepping stone, remained set in stone instead, this was not his bigger vision.

"Jimmy!" Roger called from the copy machine as Jim walked into the main floor. No one's called him Jimmy

Chapter 1

since he was 3. Only Roger. Roger looked like Santa out of costume. "It's Monday. Time to stop, pop and get stuff rollin'!" This was Roger's announcement upon Jim's entrance every morning, whether it was Monday or Friday. For some reason, Roger really liked Jim. Jim wasn't quite sure why, but it did make him feel secure.

Jim pulled out the chair from underneath his desk. He could see crumbs from his lunch the day before and noticed not-quite-adequate job done by the night cleaning crew. When he sat down, he reviewed the last thought that went through his mind. It was the same thought every day after Roger did his shtick. "Security," thought Jim. He always felt good that at least he felt secure in this job that he's had for over seven years. While others floated in and out, Jim always had this safety net of knowing he has a paycheck coming. The downside though, was that his paycheck rarely, if ever increased. If it did, it didn't satisfy the things he really wanted to do. It also didn't make him feel any different with higher numbers. Actually, he was feeling a little too secure. There was nothing to look forward to. He hung out with the same people at lunch everyday. They were pleasant, but there was no feeling of impulse. Ever. What happened to the drive that got him this 'stepping stone' job? Where did that kid from college go? The one who was going to create films that changed the world?

He looked at his inbox filled with emails about new pet rescue shelter articles he had to edit before they honorably made it onto the 'news'. Upon opening the first job, he laughed off his old ways of thinking and returned to reality. For a second there, he felt a rush just thinking back to those days. But it left just as quickly as it came.

"Monday night football at our house, bro'!" Roger exclaimed, as he placed a coffee mug on Jim's desk. He was invited every Monday night for football but he never said yes.

"I don't drink coffee, remember Roger?" Jim ignored the football question as he did being called bro' by a sixty something year old man. He assumed by now Roger must have his RSVP.

"Good stuff." Roger ignored Jim's coffee dismissal and walked away.

Jim started plugging forth at his work feeling numb to another non-stimulating conversation.

As the day ended, Jim recounted the ten or more inconsequential interactions he had with Roger, the twenty feelings of bemuse and the absence of interest, let alone passion. Like every Monday through Thursday, he turned off his computer at 5pm, grabbed his keys, threw his backpack over his shoulders, closed any open drawers and left the office to head home. He never brought work home with him because he didn't need to. There was never anything pressing or too challenging that kept him engaged. His work was easy. And life mimicked work. His bills were always paid on time because he adhered to an exact budget on a daily basis.

CHAPTER 1

Everything was always in its place. He witnessed others around him who panicked every two weeks when their paychecks couldn't support their life. He also witnessed those same people take a lot more risks than he did. While he praised his non-stressful life and responsible qualities, he envied a little something in the others.

Three months ago, he remembered Troy who lived just across the hall. Troy worked as a freelance programmer on contract jobs for websites that bored him. He decided that he really wanted to create something beyond what anyone knew him capable of doing. And he did. In a matter of months, he created something so huge he received over 100,000 hits on the video promoting it. This happened within the hour that it launched. Only three months ago Troy told Jim that he felt unfulfilled. Troy had more work than he could handle, but it was all tedious to him. It was one mundane project after the other. He said that he felt he was being unfair to himself and to his clients if he kept at it. He didn't care anymore that he could survive and make a living. He already proved that to himself. He wanted to prove something bigger to himself. He wanted to reach the potential he could feel inside.

It scared Jim in that moment to think of what Troy was doing. He moved out to live with his parents. A thirty-five year old guy, who hadn't lived at home since he was seventeen, was going back. He took his little amount of savings and put it into his big idea. He had nothing coming in that he could count on. Jim remembered this pain in his own heart. The same distress he used to get when he had to speak in front of class. It was this sharp, jerking feeling that happened when he was afraid. Those same thoughts stifled him – taking the risks that Troy did. After his conversation with Troy, Jim went back into his apartment and imagined what it would feel like to be Troy.

Unimaginably scary.

He turned on his movies, heated up some left over chili and waited for relief to wash over him. For him, this existence represented security and not going out on a limb. The interesting thing was, he felt like he was still waiting to feel alive.

When Friday came the next week, Jim was ready to zone out. Although he was jaded during most of the day at work, he could at least dream a little at home even if it did strike anxiety within. This Friday was no different than the rest. He received his paycheck, paid his bills and watched his account return to a small amount, until his next paycheck filled it up again. It seemed absurd to him. He didn't live an exuberant lifestyle. In fact, he didn't ever feel like he was really living at all. He took local transportation to work, whether the bus or train. He ate the same meals every day: English muffin with peanut butter and honey for breakfast, bologna and horseradish cheddar cheese sandwiches on cracked wheat and chili, ravioli or the occasional fast food burger for dinner. It rarely varied. He lived in an older apartment with rent lower than most. His utility bills

CHAPTER 1

ranked lower than average and his entertainment expenses consisted of renting a video game here and there, or buying a movie on Pay-Per-View. His life was simple, budgeted and ... truthfully unfulfilling.

On most nights he could drift off to sleep, excited for the escape from reality and hopeful that his imaginative mind would kick in and give him at least seven hours of adventure. But tonight, his mind was racing. There was always a level of unease and worry that accompanied thoughts of change. He became very good at hushing those thoughts and putting himself back into the mundane for the hope of peace. Why now were these thoughts not going away? It felt like a pot inside had been simmering for a while. Occasionally it would die down. Tonight, though, it felt uncontrollable. There was no control on the fire beneath it. It was beginning to bubble and it was loud. Somehow, without any knowledge, his overworked nerves exhausted his body and he fell into a deep sleep. The adventure he hoped for heard the summons and came.

His dreams were choppy like how dreams often appear. His heart was racing. His forehead perspiring. There were images being thrown about. Most importantly, these pictures brought feelings and emotions with them. His heart raced with enthusiasm; something his body only knew of now in this dream. The blood pumping from this rapid heartbeat gave him life; something else he only knew from this. Creativity, purpose and drive were rushing through him as if he'd just towered the highest peak in the world in the fastest amount of time.

Spread out on his back with his heart and mind facing the sky, his hands open upward and his mind completely engaged in deep rest and intention, Jim felt more than he had felt in many years and perhaps in his whole life. His eyes awoke just seconds before his alarm would normally wake him. But it was Saturday. There was no alarm, there was no pattering above his head. There was no catching the bus and there was no making a lunch to bring to work. He had the next two days to himself. He was invigorated by this dream. Without even knowing what it meant and what or where the pictures were, he felt something different. He experienced a sense of freedom that he could actually do something. How long this feeling would last, he didn't know. But, it was just enough to shift his mind.

On a normal Saturday, his routine would have him getting dressed early in preparation for anything that day. Nothing ever changed though. Jim did not welcome new activities or social gatherings. Instead, he sat in his apartment on a Saturday, fully clothed, reading a book or if the mood hit, playing a game that he walked down to the local gaming store to buy. Today he woke up from this dream and without putting on any decent clothes, he went straight to the drawer beneath the microwave in his kitchen that held change from his pockets, unanswered cards, phone chargers and keys. There it was. The storage key.

When Jim first moved in, he carried with him items that didn't fit in his apartment. The property manager gave him the option of renting a unit underneath the building to store any extras. He agreed and placed the items he wasn't using in there. He hadn't visited that unit since. Today he would. He took his key and squeezed it tight. He shoved his feet into some slippers by the door and headed out. When he reached the bottom floor of the building where the cars were parked, he felt a rush go through him. It was unexplainable. He passed the cars as he listened to the echo of his shuffling slippers on the concrete. There it was, located just behind the parked blue Fiat that belonged to Rori, who lived in 3B. He took out the key he held inside his warm flannel pajama pants pocket. His hands were still cold. He opened the lock and slid the door open. It was a small, attic-like space, but it served its holding purpose. When the door opened, he could smell the stale air release. He inhaled searching for the scent of the dream he once had. It was still there. Lying on its side, cradled in blue padded quilt was his 16mm camera. Just next to it was the tripod and all of its supportive equipment. A bag was stuffed behind both of them. Inside that bag were his reels. All of the short films he made as a student were in that bag.

He was instantly brought back to the ads he'd placed in the local papers and in the trades looking for free actors to play in his films in exchange for a free demo tape of their talents. He wanted to create shorts that impacted others.

He made several films he was proud of, but when the small audiences of students and family weren't receptive, he quit.

Just the thought of shoving these all back into this storage unit to hide made him feel ill. His hands weren't cold anymore. If they were, he couldn't feel it. His heart was racing again, much like it did in his dream. Only this time, it was a feeling completely opposite of enthusiasm. This rush was induced by regret. Why did he quit? Why did it feel so easy to take this job instead? Why didn't he stick to it?

Hours later, Jim found himself still wearing his pajamas and slippers. The camera sat dusted and folded on the coffee table just in front of his beige microfiber sofa. He'd been staring at it waiting to unfold it. Next to him on the couch was the bag of movies he'd made; something else he was hesitant to open. What emotions would they stir up? If it had been this difficult to retrieve these items, how difficult would it be to use them, see them, hear them and experience them all over again? Could he handle it? His mind raced again.

He stood up and stretched. He decided to shower in hopes of washing off the discomfort. It was no use. The hot water alleviated a light pressure in his shoulders. It didn't settle his mind or his nerves. He stepped out, toweled off and put on his blue jeans and an old college t-shirt. He walked past the camera again, looking at it like a peculiar artifact that must be deciphered before reporting back to his archeological team. It was hardly ancient; only to him. When

CHAPTER 1

the pressure rose from approaching the camera, he walked away again. This time he poured himself a glass of milk from his refrigerator. It tasted good. It went down smoothly and it added something to his empty stomach. He folded his arms, still holding the glass with one hand. He nodded his head and swallowed hard. His gritting teeth made two knobs on either side of his cheeks. This was it.

He set down the glass and reached for the camera. He pulled it out with vigor now. He stretched it out on all three legs. Whatever residue left on the camera made its way into his nose and he sneezed twice in a row. He wiped his nose with the back of his hand and stepped back. It looked old. The camera looked ancient to him. His mind zipped back to college standing just outside the dorms with Taz. Taz was his camera guy when he was directing. While Jim liked to film himself, he was more of the creator. When he wasn't behind the lens, he had Taz at his side to brainstorm and invent with. What ever happened to Taz? Taz was his best friend back then. He challenged Jim to get crazy with his work. They ate lunch together every day. They skipped classes to film random stints on campus and wrote scenes at coffee shops on Friday nights while everyone went out clubbing.

Jim's mind went to the last screening he held in the shared living space of his dorm suite. About fifteen people gathered. He was proud of this piece. Taz was too. It captured the hope of students, their drive and the limitations that held them back after school was over. It was everything he believed in and wanted to spread. Yet when others, all fifteen, didn't believe and didn't resonate, he shut down. Taz reminded him of their purpose and why it didn't matter what these guys thought. After all, they probably only came for the free food and drinks. They were on to something else after that viewing. They cared more about which DJ would be spinning that night than they did about Jim's vision. Whatever Taz said, Jim didn't hear it. He didn't hear it until now and it hurt.

It was time for him to pull out the reels. He never gave his VHS player away. He was partly glad and partly wished he had. He blew on away the dust and popped it inside his small television box with DVD and VHS player attached. The first thing he saw was Taz' face. He was laughing and making jokes.

"One day you will recognize us when we accept our awards for best documentary film." Taz said while trying to keep a straight face. He was a skinny kid with black hair and bright blue eyes. He was being filmed on a handheld camera. The camera was then passed onto a younger Jim with long, uncombed hair.

"Our mission is to make sure you never stop dreaming. If you do, we all lose."

Jim watched himself. He was filled with hope and determination. Where was that guy? What happened to him? His eyes started to burn. Tears made their way down his face to his surprise. He hadn't cried or felt this kind of emotion in years. Why now?

He wiped his face and stopped the film. He sat down on the couch and looked through the videos in the bag and wondered about Taz. Where was he now? What was he doing? Did he find his dreams?

By now, the sky was getting dark. Jim sat back and decided to watch every single one of these tapes. He laughed. He cried. He smiled and he thought, "What if?" What if he kept going? What if he and Taz did exactly what they said they were going to do? What if he followed his own mission?

It wasn't hard for him to find Taz. It was his own fault for not being in contact with anyone besides his parents and his boss. That night, after watching all twelve of his short films, Jim joined a social network that would give him access to his old friends. He wasn't void enough to know that if he was going to bring anything into his life, he at least needed access. Within a couple of hours, Jim had one hundred friends; one of whom was Taz.

"Hey man! What's been going on?" Taz was quick to instant message Jim upon his friend's request.

Jim was quick to hide the fact that he had done practically nothing in all these years to support what he once said he believed in. To Jim's surprise, Taz was stuck in a job that was less than satisfying to him as well. Taz was married, though, and had two children. The conversation went to the phone after a few messages back and forth.

"Ah, you know, I just keep on going 'cause I got to support this family. I mean yeah, I think back all the time and then I blow it off that we'd probably be struggling, poor and desperate for a return phone call from just one agent. We're adults now, ya know?" Taz sounded tired, not like the guy Jim once knew. His excuse was something Jim would normally buy into and probably agree with, but right now it made no sense to him at all.

"Why did we give it up Taz?" Jim pushed.

"Jim, I would have stuck with you, but you were done. You got your other gigs for other people and you wanted to please your parents. You were dating Liz at the time and she didn't really support your dreams." Taz was right. Jim forgot about Liz. It wasn't just his family and the other students. Liz praised him for getting a job as a writer and shunned his independent ideas. An entrepreneur to her was someone who couldn't get a real job. Jim bought into that. No sooner did he take the job, did she leave because Jim "wasn't the same anymore."

"What happened to Liz anyway, Jim?" Taz asked.

"She married a musician. The guy travels all over the world and they have houses in three different countries."

"Ha. Interesting." Taz replied. "Well, he was lucky."

"Is it luck Taz? I'm still working for the same paper. And I'll be honest with you. I'm bored out of my mind. It does nothing for me. I can never move up because there's nowhere to go."

CHAPTER 1

There was silence on the other end of the line and Jim thought for a moment that Taz was relating to him. "I broke out the camera and all of our short films today." Jim could hear Taz sigh on the other end of the line.

"Those days are gone Jim." Taz responded.

This made Jim's heart break a little. The guy that used to be filled with all "yeses" and zero "nos" drained the hope left in Jim. "Do they have to be?" Jim asked.

"Dude, what's this really about? Why are you now connecting after all these years?" Taz wasn't dumb.

"I need to make a change, man. Last night I had this dream and it was invigorating. I was making a difference. I was helping other people make a difference. This morning I woke up realizing I didn't want to just feel that in a dream. I want it to be real. I don't want to die without having that feeling. I don't care where I end up, if I fail, if I succeed. I just want that feeling back. I want other people to have that feeling. I can make money. I can support myself. But, I don't feel what success is supposed to feel like. I feel stuck, Taz. I don't want to be stuck."

Taz was quiet again. After a few moments, he responded, "I don't want to be stuck either, man."

"We told ourselves quitting on our dream was selfish. To keep our talents locked away wouldn't serve anyone. It would be taking away instead of giving. So why are we taking away? Why are you taking away from your kids?" Jim was convincing himself as he was convincing Taz.

"All right, man," he paused. "Let's do it."

"Really?!"

"Really!" Taz was feeling it now. "I want to be an example to my kids. I want to show them why we're here."

Jim laughed out loud. The old feelings were coming back.

"So what do we do?" Taz asked.

"We gotta start. We take weekends and we film. We capture people, wherever they are at in their life. Let's document real people on their own mission." Jim was pumped. "You be my camera guy? I'll direct?"

"You're sure about this?"

"What do we have to lose?"

Jim, took all of the next day, Sunday, to prepare for this journey. He knew he would have to use all of his spare time he was currently doing nothing with, to make this happen. He made a list of places to find people. He was going to get to the bottom of how people rise to the top. What makes them keep going? How do they succeed when they start with nothing?

Chapter 2

DRIVING INTERVENTION

Jim was awake long before the alarm went off. Even if he was going to a job he wasn't jazzed about, he now had something that motivated him and was going to make everything he did that day more enjoyable. Well, almost everything....

He didn't quite expect his morning to go as it did. As soon as he arrived at work, there was a different energy. It may have something to do with his new perspective. In any case, it must be more recognizable now that he felt inspired. But that wasn't it. Even though he might not be jovial coming into work each day, he at least noticed others who actually were satisfied with their jobs. So, what was different this time?

"Hey, where's the big guy?" Jim asked Meghan who answered the phones at reception.

"I doubt he's coming in," Meghan replied.

"Is there something going on that I don't know about?" Jim was confused now. Roger never missed a day of work.

Even when he was sick, he loved being Editor in Chief and conversing with his staff so much that he came in.

"You didn't get the email over the weekend?" Meghan asked.

"What email?" Jim didn't get the email because Jim never checked his work email on the weekends. In fact, he never even set up remote access to get into the server at work. He never missed deadlines and there was never anything to be done.

"They're taking him out. They're merging with another paper. You either got an offer to stay with the new company for less pay or you got the boot."

Jim walked away and went to his desk. He opened his emails. Meghan was right. There it was, simply stated. He could take less pay and keep his job with the merger or he could move on. Apparently Roger gave him high reviews because it was stated in the letter that he was considered to be of high value to the paper. Jim couldn't understand why. There was nothing about writing his brief notifications to the people of Philly that seemed difficult. He was appreciative of Roger's praise of him, but he didn't find relief in the offer. Some people at the office were just relieved to have a job, while others panicked to find another.

The timing of this announcement couldn't have been more scripted. It was as if his request for something different this weekend was delivered first priority to some higher force and paid upon request. This wasn't quite the way Jim wanted it to go. While he wasn't ecstatic about his position with the paper, he would at least have some security and money coming in to feed this new project. To stay at a job he didn't like for less pay now? Jim had a rush of feelings that he couldn't quite grasp. What was he going to do now?

The day carried on as usual and new people came at different hours talking to some of the employees. One of the women, who was tall and quite elegant looking, called upon everyone's attention just after lunch, "Thank you for your patience and cooperation during this fast-paced change. For those of you staying with us, we have organized a meeting tomorrow morning for you all to attend. Thank you." Everyone shuffled back to their desks looking like the jilted person on the V8 commercial who didn't drink their juice.

The same woman made her way to Jim's desk. "You must be Jim?"

"Uh, yes, hi."

"Hi Jim. I'm Laura Mischner. I'll be meeting with you today to discuss the changes. Can we step into the conference room?" She held out her hand.

"Sure."

"Great, I'll be waiting."

Jim stood up and pushed his chair in, feeling very uneasy about all of this. He watched Laura walk to the conference room, dressed in a beige tweed suit, stockings and low patent leather heels. He questioned why she was so formal. He walked in just after her. She asked if he would like water or coffee and he politely declined. It was interesting to him how comfortable she was in making this her space. He suddenly felt so out of place.

"So, Jim. Roger has told us many great things about you."

"Where is Roger?"

She was stumped by his quick response. "Well, as you know we have acquired this paper and while the paper will still run as it is, we are now the ones that own it."

"Why is that? Roger never warned us."

"Well, it's probably best kept within the leaders of the company."

Ouch. Now, Jim knew for sure, he wasn't comfortable. "So Jim, we'd love for you to stay. I don't assume you have other options at this point. Unfortunately for the sake of the company, we won't be able to keep you at your current salary, but we can increase it based on performance in the following six months. I imagine it won't be long until you return to your previous pay."

Was she being serious? In that moment, Jim pulled himself back to look at this situation. It was so clear to him. If he stayed here, he would be pulling himself further away from his dream. Nothing about this felt aligned with his conversation with Taz. Nothing.

"I imagine the work isn't too difficult, so it shouldn't be long before…"

"I'm sorry," Jim interrupted. "I am actually not interested in maintaining my position here."

Laura froze. She was confused. Everyone, everywhere, as far as she knew was desperate to keep their jobs. "You're not interested?"

"Correct." Jim stood up. "I appreciate you taking this time, but I'll be collecting my things and moving out shortly."

Laura sat with complete confusion on her face. Jim wouldn't know because he never looked back. He simply went to his desk, packed his things and said his goodbyes to the rest of the staff.

Something struck him in that moment that caused him to walk away from something that felt seemingly secure, but outright incongruent with Jim. It was Maria. As soon as he opened the doors to his past and what he once dreamed of, it was as if the memories were unlocked and emotion started to make its way in again. It was this strange feeling of clarity, excitement and complete astonishment all at the same time. But he liked it.

He walked into his apartment and dropped the box containing items from his desk on the floor. He dug through his reels looking for something in particular. There it was. He pulled it out and inserted it into the player. In seconds he could see her face and it all came rushing back.

On the television monitor he could hear his younger voice. As the camera lifted he saw Maria Gamb. They were laughing and he was getting ready to count her in. "Three, two, one... hi, Maria," Jim said off camera.

Sitting on a chair just in front of a tree, Maria smiled. She had a beautiful face with short hair to frame her cheek bones. She was confident and fun. "Hi, Jim," she smiled.

"So, you know why we are filming this?"

"I do," she agreed.

"What was it that you just told me?"

"Ah, well, everything always works out for Maria."

"How do you figure?" Jim asked.

"Because your circumstance isn't your identity."

Jim paused for a moment. He thought about where he was in this moment. While he wasn't fired, he was out of a job. He didn't know whether he did the right thing or not, he just knew that staying there didn't feel right. He pressed play again, searching for something powerful Maria said on this tape that made him rush home to watch it. "I got paid each month for a job I didn't like." It was coming now. Jim could feel it.

"It was a great job. But, for someone else."

"How do you know whether it's the right job or not?" Jim asked.

"Look at your highest values. Ask yourself what you want to surround yourself with. Then see if what you are doing aligns with that. If you aren't aligned, remember that you get to choose what you want to invest in. The only thing stopping you is the courage to drive the intention." The frame stopped on her last words.

Jim watched the screen and could remember that day. Maria was so simple and straightforward in what she said to Jim. Maria was the first and only interview Jim captured for that film he wanted to make. After she spoke, he set down that camera and thanked her. He was so fresh at that time and so full of hope. He believed wholeheartedly in everything that she said and yet, somehow he ended up here. He was now so many years away from that dream. He realized all this time he wasn't surrounded by his highest values. But, he also knew what those values were. He was trading paper for something he believed in. Why? Even when he tried to present meaningful articles, he was shut down. They weren't interested. As much as he was liked, they saw him as one thing and one thing only. Why did he adopt the same identity? Whatever the reason, it became less important as he stared at the freeze frame of Maria's face. Now was his time. Whether he fails or succeeds, it's at least time to go.

Chapter 3

THE ICEBERG MELTS

A week passed since Jim left his job. He didn't have much in savings. He could probably get by for a couple months and then he didn't know what he would do. He figured he would collect unemployment while he decided. Taz didn't have much either and was still set on keeping his job working the cameras for a studio in New York City. Taz commuted from the suburbs each day into work. Now that Jim was out of work, they agreed he would be the one to come in on the weekends and meet Taz in the city. For now, weekends would be their only time.

Jim took the train in this Friday night and Taz met him with his two children. They laughed as soon as they saw each other and embraced in a hug the way two best friends reuniting would.

"You look great. Haven't changed too much!" Jim noticed Taz was still thin and had all his hair.

"We're not that old you know?" Taz smirked. "You don't look so bad yourself."

"I'll take it as a compliment." The two got in Taz' car and explained to Taz' three year old boy and seven year old daughter how they knew each other so well.

"Why don't you still make movies daddy? You have cameras at work." Lily asked getting excited to see her dad so pumped up.

"Well, baby, that's why Jim is out here. We're going to start doing just that."

"Cartoons!" Miles asked with his high-pitched voice.

"Not quite," Taz responded.

They enjoyed the ride to Taz' house where they were all greeted by Taz' wife, Emily. She had a complete meal prepared for them all. Jim immediately looked at the table and took note that from this day forward, he would break the old habits that weren't working and start new ones. It would begin with a delicious meatloaf and potatoes dinner with cheesecake for dessert. He felt good and he was ready to move forward.

Jim and Taz stayed up late that night planning out how this whole film would go. One thing they agreed upon was that they were rusty when it came to this and they would learn as they went.

"Let's just get some tape," Jim said.

"Tomorrow morning bright and early, we've got one stop to make and then let's go."

"What kind of a stop?" Jim asked.

"Remember my Uncle Danny?"

"Sure. He helped us buy our first camera."

"Right. Well, one of his friends is in town and he was insistent on you and I talking to him before we get started. That cool with you?"

"Heck yeah. Let's do it." Jim felt like he was 18 again.

The following morning, Jim was again awake before he needed to be. He showered and sat ready to go. Taz and Jim headed out to the big city where they would first have breakfast with a man they'd never met, but felt inclined to meet.

Walking into the big deli style restaurant, Jim saw one man sitting at a table. His hair was brown and he was very put together. His eyes looked up and met Jim's. "Taz?" The man asked.

"Oh I'm Jim," he held his hand out.

"I'm Taz." The man gave Taz a hug immediately.

"Taz! After all this time, I finally meet you. Your uncle is one heck of a guy. A true friend. I'm Aaron. Aaron Young."

"Yes he is, thank you. And well, thank you for taking the time to speak to us. Uncle Dan said you had something important to share with us."

They all sat back down at the table. "You know your uncle told me what you were both doing and I knew I had to talk to you." He took a drink of his water. "You know I've learned something from my experiences that I'd love to pass on to you both."

"Please." They both agreed.

"Sometimes everything you perceived as an established fact in your life can be changed in an instant. Sometimes the panic of it can make you feel stuck."

Taz and Jim looked at each other and nodded their heads. He was right. "Whether it's health, financial situations, relationships, or from what I see, just realizing your capabilities," Aaron continued. "When that happens, you get to decide where you want to go. I know people that have lost jobs, marriages, money and even their freedom. They might not have had a choice in the matter, but what they did have a choice in was their attitude."

"I walked out on my job for this," Jim blurted out. "And I'm not sure if it was the smart choice, but I felt like I had to."

Aaron smiled, "Then it was the right choice. You know life is less about a series of things that happen to us. But, if you can understand that the iceberg will always melt then you don't have to feel stuck."

"How do you mean?" Jim asked.

"Throughout your life you've been given opportunities. You've met different people along the way and you had the choice of how you responded to each and every one of them. From that you were given gifts." Aaron exuded strength in his words.

"Well, I don't know about gifts."

"See that's just it. It's all a gift."

CHAPTER 3

"Really? I feel like I've missed out on so much because I listened to other people. I did things I thought was right by their standards and not my own. I feel like I missed out on all of the gifts."

"That's where I disagree," Aaron said shaking his head. "Those were your tests. Maybe you didn't pass the way you wanted and so now you continue to be tested again and you will continue to be tested beyond this. But have you learned?"

Jim got it now. "Yeah, I see what you mean now," he paused and then, "I feel really excited about all of this, but so scared at the same time. I've got to stretch out two months of savings until this is made. I have to learn the business and at the same time create something. It's this feeling of immense pressure weighing on me. It's like having everything and nothing at the same time."

"It will melt. The iceberg always melts." Aaron said.

"Wait... what?" Jim asked.

"You are now set on a path to make a dream come true. You're growing and you will reap the rewards. But, whether it happens instantly or gradually, it is still happening. You will look back and realize how far you have come. It's like an iceberg melting. Little by little the pressure of the iceberg will melt. Sometimes just a small piece will melt and it's enough to break off a big piece. Sometimes, it will feel like it's happening slowly. But, look back on the past few months and see how much has changed. You realized how much is really possible. "

Jim took a deep breath looking at the bigger picture and what the end results might be because of this choice he made. "What do I do if I'm faced with the same obstacles?"

"And you will. Look, change is always scary and sometimes really painful. But, you work through it and know that the hard parts will get lighter. Every time you feel pain or struggle, know that the discomfort is bringing you closer. You are growing and achieving. Just stay confident in the dream and you will accomplish it."

Jim left that restaurant and thought about Aaron on the way to their first location. "You know as scared as I am, I feel happy that I am feeling anything at all," he told Taz.

"I know what you mean. I miss being nervous about our screenings. I miss having to figure out how to fix the lighting not knowing what we were doing. There was something about it." Taz remembered.

Jim looked over at Taz who had both hands tight on the wheel. "I felt nothing for so long Taz. Nothing. I thought being uncomfortable or scared meant it was wrong. I'm starting to believe differently."

Taz nodded his head and looked onto the road. "Me too, man. Me too.

Chapter 4

LEAP AND IT WILL ARRIVE

"Who's our first guy?" Jim asked.

"Well, we planned on finding a bunch of them randomly I know. But, I've met a good selection of people while working at the studio and I thought this guy would be a great start. His name is Greg Ausley and he's got this really cool thing going on. You'll see." Taz explained.

"Great, let's roll."

Taz and Jim walked inside the office space, carrying their equipment. They waited for Greg in the lobby.

"That's him," Taz said as soon as tall guy came walking out. "Hey, man. What's up?"

"How are you? Been a while," Greg said receiving Taz' hug.

"Greg this is Jim. Jim, Greg."

"Great to meet you," Jim smiled back.

"So, you're the guy that Taz is getting all excited about. Just a week ago he calls me up and tells me he's going to make a documentary. I used to be in film school myself.

Next thing I know he's asking me to be your first interview. I'm happy to be a part of this. Tell me more."

"Well, I want to feature real people achieving something great. I want the audience to see firsthand where they're at and what keeps them going. I'm on a rise. At least I hope I am and if I can learn from filming this and together, Taz and I can bring people like you aboard to share your insight and knowledge of how you got where you are and where you are going, I think we can make a difference. Everyone has a different story and I want to compile all of these perceptions into one amazing piece. From there… who knows?"

"You're on a good start. I like what you guys are doing and I'm happy to participate in this. Come with me. I've got a great set up for this." Greg straightened his pants and led the guys into a small room that with soft colors, a leather chair and window overlooking the city. "Will this work?"

"It's fantastic!" Jim exclaimed.

Jim and Taz might have been a little rusty getting the camera and lighting set up, but after a few minutes, they picked it up as if they were in college again.

"Are we ready?" Jim asked Taz.

"We're rolling."

After slating the name and date, Jim was ready. "Greg, you have an online company that you created to help people stay accountable for what they say they are going to do. How did one idea become so successful?"

"It's easy. Someone once told me to leap and it will arrive." Greg didn't have to think at all.

"What does that mean? How did you do it?"

"I made goals and I put all I had into making them happen because that is what gets results. Most people will gauge success on immediate results. But success doesn't always play out like that. You've got to put in the effort, knowing what the end result will be. I'm an entrepreneur at heart. I love to build things. In doing so, I've seen people quit when it's all about to fall apart. That's when I get really ramped up. I give it my all and that's when the biggest deals have happened. I won't run and hide. I will keep moving forward. Once, I take the leap, it always arrives. Be careful to have the right team with you because those moments happen when you want to walk away. But, it's those that stick with it that collect the rewards."

"And cut."

"Wow, I needed to hear that," Jim said. Even though he had just begun he couldn't help but wonder how long he would stick with this. It was as if there was a clock ticking as to how long he could hang in. He couldn't do it before, what would make this time different?

Jim quickly realized something with Greg. This film wasn't just about inspiring others to achieve, it was really about him.

"Thank you, Greg."

"You know I like what you guys are doing and I'm anxious to see how it turns out. Do me a favor and stick with it. If you do, I'll feature your story and film with my company."

"Ah, man that would be awesome."

"You've taken the leap. Keep going alright?"

Chapter 5

BOUNCY BALL

Jim stayed the weekend at Taz' house and took the train back to his place on Sunday evening. Before he left, Taz questioned why he would stay in Philadelphia at all. He urged Jim to move out to New York. It made perfect sense to Jim. What didn't make sense was how he could afford it. He opened his mailbox when he got home. He didn't care much this week for the mail or anything about the life he had there. He wanted to get out. The only thing that held his interest was Julia and Nathan upstairs and he barely had a relationship with them. There was nothing keeping him there. He didn't have two weeks to finish out his job. He chose to leave.

When he returned to his apartment with a stack of mail, he saw the stack of bills that he would have to pay to support this life – a life he was less enthused about and really, downright bored with. What seemed to excite Jim, though, was that instead of it just being boring, he was actually feeling disgusted with it. While it wasn't a good feeling, it was enough to make him want to change it.

Jim calculated the amount of money it would cost for him to stay another month. It made him sick to his stomach. It was as if he was throwing it away. Suddenly a spur of energy infused him and he went to his computer to start looking at apartments all over New York. He looked in Brooklyn, where Taz was currently living the suburbia life and things were far less expensive than the big city. He looked on the east side, the west side, he looked in surrounding suburbs and not long after the spur of energy, his energy dropped. Questions started to flood his mind. What was he doing? Was this ridiculous? What were the chances of him really making something of this film? Who would care? Why should they care? Did he care enough? Did he make a mistake? He had stability all these years. A place to sleep. Food to eat. A job. Did he already have it all? The confusion was overwhelming. He hadn't experienced such emotions since he was a senior in college. For the last decade he was flat out uninterested in anything to do with anything. Suddenly an old dream resurfaces and he can't figure out whether he really does like feeling the ups and downs or if he'd rather go back to feeling nothing. Could he win?

The intense high of doing something new and living on the edge was quickly turning into panic and finally depression. Jim didn't want to play his games or watch a movie. He didn't even want to eat. Looking at apartments and seeing reality was making him feel ill and tired.

The beginning of that week Jim spent most of his days in bed with the curtains drawn. He avoided calls and he avoided life. He wondered for a moment if this was comparable to a rock bottom. Nothing seemed clear to him. Just days ago, it seemed he was completely inspired. Maria did it. Aaron did it. And Greg was holding him accountable.

Just at that thought, Jim shot up in bed and looked around. He noticed the pile of clothes on the floor and the dark feel of the room. "This isn't home anymore," he said out loud.

He picked up his phone and called Taz right away.

"Dude, what's going on? I've been trying to get you. Are you ok?" Taz sounded worried and angry at the same time.

"I'm fine. I just had a setback."

"Look man, why don't you come stay with us for a while. You can bunk here until you sort things out. We're in this together, right?"

Jim smiled. Taz was right. "Yes. Yes, I will come stay with you. Thank you," he broke for a moment. "Really. Thank you."

"Thank me after you get your butt here. We've got an amazing woman scheduled on Saturday. I ran into her on one of the show's tapings. She's only in town until Sunday. I need you man. She's good. And I have a feeling she's going to help you too."

Jim rebooted and remembered the reason he was doing this. He recollected that he was the one that needed to care most about this. If he could do that, the right people would follow.

He didn't have much in his apartment and it took all of one full day for him to pack things up. He gathered used boxes from the dumpster and Julia was kind enough to help him get rid of some things he couldn't use anymore. He listed his furniture for sale and was able to fit everything else in his car.

In two days, Jim was in route to Brooklyn to stay with Taz. He smiled and sang the whole way there. It was early Saturday morning when he arrived at their house. He dropped off his things in the basement, where he would be staying. It had a small kitchen and bathroom built in. He needed nothing else. By lunchtime Taz and Jim were on their way to meet with Savannah Brooklyn Ross, an incredible woman who was well known for being the number one top real-estate investor in Canada, but even more so, was her story of determination and how she got there after almost losing her son.

"Some people get stuck on how they are supposed to reach their success." Jim was on camera with Savannah and Taz behind the lens. Savannah sat back, very relaxed. Jim knew immediately this was an authentic woman. He admired her ability to just tell it like it is with complete sincerity.

"What do they get stuck on?" Jim asked.

"They won't entertain different vehicles. Sometimes it's not the plane that's going to get there. Sometimes it's the pogo stick. But, a lot of people say, 'I won't take the pogo stick!' and so they have a harder time getting where they want to go and often times don't get there at all. They won't accept that it might be hard to get there and they also don't accept when it's too easy."

Jim could see that in his own life right away. "Why do you think people do that?"

"Because they aren't focused enough on where they are going and they don't open themselves up to who and what can get them there. They get stuck in the lows not realizing the bounce."

"The bounce?" Taz poked his head out while still holding the camera steady.

"Oh yeah. If you take a bouncy ball and you drop it from the top of a high staircase, it will come right back up. In fact, the lower you drop it the higher it bounces back. If people could see themselves as that ball, they wouldn't let the challenges and the drops hold them back."

Jim paused for a moment and thought about his own recent drops. He knew that those drops had to happen if was going to bounce any distance. Savannah watched Jim take it in and continued, "You can't hit the top unless you've hit the bottom. I know this first hand."

"How do you know if you've hit rock bottom?"

"It's different for everyone. The point is that you let yourself breakdown and breakthrough. Let yourself feel the emotion, the anger, the sadness, the fear, and the pain. When you can allow yourself to feel that, then you can breakthrough and you can rise."

A tear came to Jim's eye. Taz saw it and smiled. He zoomed in on it and then the hug that Jim couldn't hold himself back from giving. He then looked at Taz who was still filming, "You were right. She came just at the right time." He then looked back at Savannah who had tears herself. She knew exactly what he was feeling. "Thank you."

"Oh no. Thank you," she said. Jim and Taz quickly noticed these interviews were going to be powerful once they were compiled and edited. The vision for the whole project was getting bigger and it was starting to feel so big that Jim could hardly keep up with his own racing thoughts. It took him awhile to get to sleep that night, but when he finally did, he felt peace. Somewhere inside, he had the confidence and the persistence to see this through and each day it would get stronger, even with the setbacks.

Chapter 6

PLAY UP YOUR LIMITATIONS

"I'm starving. This is going to be such a treat. I really appreciate this." Jim and Taz walked into an American Steak House restaurant located right in the heart of Manhattan. Taz took his wife there on special occasions and he argued that since they had not yet properly celebrated their new venture, they were owed this meal.

"Yeah, of course. Just wait until you try the food. It's out of this world." Taz looked over at the chalkboard displaying in perfect penmanship the specials for the evening. "Oh, look at that!"

"What?" Jim asked.

"Rick Gresh is the guest chef tonight. That guy's amazing. He's from Chicago. I went there with Emily for one of her conferences and we ate at his restaurant. I thought we were in for a treat before; I think we just hit the jackpot."

"I'm in!"

About a half hour later, Jim and Taz were barely speaking to each other. The only sounds coming from their mouth were the ooohs, aaahs, mmm's and oh my God this is good.

Finally after his last bite, Jim said, "We've got to speak to this chef. Food like this can't go unnoticed."

"I'm sure he's been requested by every table. But, what's the harm in asking?" Taz made eye contact with their server and waved him over.

"How are you gentlemen doing?" The young man was polite as one would expect at a fine dining establishment.

"Fantastic. The food is amazing. I'm sure he's busy and gets asked a lot, but is there any chance we could thank the chef personally?" Jim responded.

"I'll see what I can do."

"We'd really appreciate it," Taz added.

"In the meantime, is there anything else I can get you both?"

"I'd love a cappuccino," Taz answered. "You still a non-coffee drinker?" He asked Jim.

"Still no coffee, but I'd love a dessert menu."

"You got it. Be right back with that," the waiter said. He grabbed some empty dishes and headed off.

Jim was well into his dessert and Taz was taking the last sip of his cappuccino when the guest chef, Rick, made his appearance. Jim and Taz were taken aback when he approached the table.

"Wow, are you Chef Rick?" Taz said.

Chapter 6

"What gave it away, the chef jacket or the tattoos?" Rick joked.

"We figured you'd be too busy," Taz laughed.

"I'm always busy, but never too busy. This is what I love." Rick replied.

"We can't tell you how much we enjoyed this."

"I'm so glad to hear that. It's always a challenge when I'm working in a new kitchen. But, I must say, it's been a great night. The staff has really embraced my ideas."

"What do you mean?"

"A lot of restaurants seem to forget that it's all about the guests. We worked hard getting the team together tonight, making sure that everything we do leads to an unforgettable experience for you as a guest."

"We certainly noticed that in the presentation and even in the taste. My wife and I have been coming here for years and I have to say this is one of the best times I've had here. I'm sorry she missed it. Glad I didn't though!" Taz smiled.

"I'm so glad you like it. The head chef, Thomas is a frequent diner at my place in Chicago. He invited me out to spend a couple of nights working in their kitchen and I never turn down a trip to New York."

"Believe it or not, I've been there. I was so happy to see you would be here tonight."

"Oh, great. Please make sure to say hello the next time you're there."

"Absolutely."

Jim looked around the restaurant. "Well, by the looks of it, people are lucky if they have just a two hour wait. I'm glad we had a reservation." They all laughed.

Jim could feel the conversation coming to a close, but something prompted him to ask Rick more questions. "Do you mind if I ask you something?"

"Sure, go right ahead." Rick said.

"Did you always have others support your dream?"

Rick laughed almost immediately. "I'll tell you what. The people I thought I needed the most support from were restauranteurs and investors. It's actually the people that really knew me: my family, friends and the crew I worked with day in and day out that were the most important."

"You know what we need?" Taz interrupted.

"Camera." Jim supplied. He looked up at Rick, "I know you're a busy man tonight and this is probably way out of line, but my buddy here and I are making a film about the journey of the rise – rising to the top. We've been interviewing all sorts of people and I feel like you would make a great addition to this documentary."

Rick smiled and said, "I am busy and it's a little difficult on a night like this, but I'll tell you what. You give me five minutes to check on the kitchen and I'm all yours. There's an office in the back where we can film."

Jim looked around, "If I can be honest, I think right here amidst the mayhem of salivating patrons is perfect."

Rick shrugged his shoulders. "Alright then! Be back in five." He rushed off to take care of business.

About five minutes later, Rick returned at the same time Taz came back with the camera from the car. As Taz was setting up, Jim noticed the customers watching with curious eyes.

"Dang it!" Taz blurted out.

"What's up?" Jim asked.

"Ah, just having a hard time getting the film roll right. This camera is pretty old."

Jim looked at Rick starting to feel embarrassed. "Sorry about that. Can't afford a new camera yet, so we're making this off my old college cam."

"Embrace what you have," Rick said in a very calm voice that was the distinct opposite from the anxiety-filled voices Taz and Jim just adopted.

Jim looked at him in question. Rick didn't need him to say anything, he just continued, "Look at the big picture. Are you looking for something immediate or long term?"

"Got it," Taz got the camera rolling and was eager to capture every word.

"Long term," Jim replied.

"Play up your limitations," Rick returned. Taz zoomed in on Rick's face at that moment and then moved the camera to Jim who shyly looked into the camera as if he was caught. He squinted his eyes for a moment while he looked at Rick. He then looked at Taz who put his lips together and nodded.

"That's what I did," Rick continued through the silence. "I didn't have a lot of money when I got started. I didn't have a lot of knowledge, but I was sure good at cooking." Taz zoomed out to capture Jim listening to Rick. "I looked at the things I wasn't so good at and I sort of played it up. I was making gourmet food in a not so gourmet kitchen or setting and it didn't matter. What I soon found out was that playing up what I thought were limitations actually brought me more attention. That's when the positive really showed. Suddenly I was able to shine because I wasn't hiding from what I didn't have."

Jim nodded his head, "This camera is pretty old school." They all laughed.

"Use it! People will love it. They love rooting for the unlikely guy, the underdog, the one who isn't expected to win. Make a vintage style documentary. You're using the same camera you started the dream with. You think people won't love that?" Rick raised his eyebrows.

Jim looked in the camera just then, "This film just got a whole lot better."

Taz stopped rolling.

Chapter 7

TO DO LIST

"Thank you for your time and we'll let you know of the release party," Jim said as he took a man's card and put it into his back pocket.

"Not bad for a random off the street," Taz said as he brought the camera down from his shoulder. The two started to head back to their car.

"Making a movie?" A woman's voice coming out of two glass doors just near their car asked.

"Huh?" Jim was standing at the parking meter and heard the voice behind him. When he turned around he saw a tall attractive blonde woman standing there. "Oh yeah, we're making a movie about people; where they're at, where they're going, where they want to go and how they're getting there."

"What made you decide to do this?" She asked.

"Do you mind?" Taz popped up behind her with his camera.

"You have some type of contract with the people you film?" She figured these guys were filming everything.

"Of course," Jim responded quickly.

"Alright, let's get that out of the way and we'll shoot."

Her name was Lori Taylor and she was an expert in marketing, social media and everything to do with public relations. One thing the guys knew for sure. This woman was sharp.

She signed quickly and had no concern about how she looked. It surprised the guys, since she was a beautiful woman. They figured she would want a touch up before being on camera. But she was less concerned with her hair and more concerned with what the intention of this film was and she had an interesting way of finding out.

"So, tell me why you're doing this?" She didn't forget her question either.

"Well, we want people to see what real people are doing--"

"No. I mean you. Why are *you* doing this?" Her eyes locked onto Jim's, who froze immediately. He tried to cover it with a laugh while praying at the same time he had the same confidence as a Morgan Spurlock that could run any conversation. "Um, because I want to make a difference."

"Well, they all say that, don't they?" Could Jim get nothing by this woman? Did he not have a good enough reason? What was his reason? In about two seconds flat all those emotions filled with doubt and fear came rolling in and now on top of it – humiliation.

"Don't be embarrassed," she said.

How did she know he was embarrassed?

"Yeah man, it's making you real red right now and it's not looking good through the lens." Taz could see Jim's discomfort. Jim shot Taz a look that was an obvious question of their friendship.

"No, you look great." She laughed. "But, really. What's in this for you?"

Jim kept thinking about the message of the film and how it could inspire others. He knew he was starting to learn from these people, but he didn't really see it as a self-serving project. "I wanted this to be for everyone else."

"You said that. But, what's in it for you?"

"I want to create. I want to do something that matters and writing about the new hardware store opening up on 5th and Washington was boring me."

Lori smiled. "Ok, I'm starting to get it now. You must have liked something about that job, right?"

Jim thought for a minute. "Well, yeah. I liked it when I could make community announcements in a funny way. I liked seeing things happen for other people, but most of the time to be honest, I was jealous that they were making their dreams come true. Whether it was opening up a sandwich shop, getting married or saving a park, those people smiled about what they did. I wasn't smiling that often."

"Are you smiling more now?"

"Apparently I'm blushing now! The attention is supposed to be on the people we interview, not me."

"But, this is your journey right? This is technically your… what did you call this? Rise?"

Jim slowly smiled with admission, "I guess so."

"Tell me your name?"

"Jim."

"Jim?" she clarified and he nodded in return. "What do you want?"

Jim took a deep breath and looked in the camera, "I guess this one's about me." He looked to the ground and started to think.

"Hey I practically invited myself into this conversation, why not make it about you? What do you want?" She was determined and Jim couldn't understand why.

"I want to feel good about something I've done."

"Ok, that's cool," she agreed while nodding her head. "What don't you want?"

Jim sighed, "Well, I don't want to feel useless and like I wasted my life. I don't want to panic about what I'm going to do with my life and how I'm going to survive. I don't want to fail. I don't want to feel overwhelmed or confused or inadequate." He let it out like a whoopee cushion releases air, fast and noisy.

They all paused in reaction.

"Wow." Lori just looked at him with wide eyes. "You got a lot of things on your To Don't list and ignored your To Do list."

Jim's cheeks were getting hot again. She was right. He had to brainstorm what he wanted. But, when it came to what he didn't want, he was like an unstoppable rocket.

"Make your To Do list longer. Focus on those things instead of all the embarrassment, fear, doubt, and helplessness. You're your own boss now Jim, right?"

"Yeah, I guess so."

"Then make that list what you want it to be and *get* it!" She went to her purse and pulled out her keys. "Well, I gotta get going guys. Thanks for letting me in. It was fun. Let me know when it's done, I'll help you out with getting it seen." She started to walk away.

"Wait, we never interviewed you--," Jim called after her. But she was already a distance away. She held up her hand and waved. "I got my point across."

When Taz and Jim got in the car, Jim took the camera and held it in front of him to film while they were driving. "I think I finally realized why I'm doing this." He then turned the camera to Taz. "You?"

"Oh I know why I'm doing this," Taz said while looking at the road. He then turned to the camera, "I'm just happy you know now. Things are about to get good." Jim turned the camera to the road and turned up the music.

Chapter 8

POWER OF THREE

"That's the secret to changing the world." Jim heard a man say as he and Taz walked along the streets of New York. He turned to Taz.

"Did you hear that?" He asked Taz.

"Did he say the secret to changing the world?" Taz heard it too. They both turned around and headed back to a young guy standing outside a music shop. "Whether he's got it or not. We've got to talk to this guy."

Jim and Taz waited while the young guy with long blonde hair finished a conversation with a young woman. She gave him a big hug goodbye. Without having to take notice, he walked right over to Jim and Taz as if he were waiting to speak with them. "I'm Jake. Jake Ducey." He held out his hand. It was so strange to Jim and Taz. It was as if this meeting was set up. They went along with it. "I notice you guys have a camera there. It's an older model, sweet!"

"Yeah we're making a film filled with messages from people like you," Jim volunteered.

"Yes, and it's also about helping this guy achieve a dream of making a movie." Taz nudged Jim.

"You are dead set on embarrassing me, aren't you?" Jim sneered at Taz.

"Right on. How can I help?" Jake asked.

"Well, we couldn't help but overhear about a secret you have."

"Yeah. I found it to be pretty congruent with anyone who's left a big mark in history. It's something that they've lived by and if we can do the same, well then watch out." Jake was very confident in his words.

"Really? I'm intrigued. Can we film you?" Jim asked.

"Absolutely."

Jim hopped in front of the camera before asking Jake more questions and slated, "This is Jim MacDonald standing here with Jake…"

"Ducey," Jake filled in with a smile on his face.

"We are about to find out a secret and we promise to give Jake full credit of this secret." He looked over to Jake. "That good?"

He laughed. "Yeah, that's great."

Jim spoke to the camera, "So, as you all know, we started this venture to follow people along their rise to whatever it is that will bring them fulfillment. It wasn't until a recent interview that I realized; maybe this was about me finding others for my own rise. And since I am on this rise and part of that rise is finding out why I am doing this, I couldn't help but stop in my tracks when I heard," he looked to Jake, "Can you tell them what I heard?"

Jake smiled, "Yeah, I was telling a young beautiful woman who was about to make a big change in her life that the equation to changing the world and your own life lies in the power of three."

"What's the power of three?" Jim asked.

"It's pretty simple, actually. But of course, simple isn't always easy, right?"

Jim agreed.

"Well, let me explain it this way. Everyone has an operating system. The Power of Three is a blueprint for people to have anything they want, and live a life of ultimate fulfillment. Whether you're already successful and want improvement, or don't know where to start, there are three short steps so that you can go anywhere you want, as long as it's for the highest good of all."

Jim was a little skeptical. This young guy seemed very sure and Jim figured that if something was simple, maybe it wasn't legit. But, maybe he was wrong. He continued to listen while Taz captured Jake.

"The first power is passion. The second is power itself and the third is purpose. That's the equation to change. That's the Power of Three. But, you have to look at it like it's urgent."

"Urgent?" Jim asked. He gave the camera a pondering eye.

"It is urgent. It's urgent that you maximize your passion, power and purpose and that you spread it to everyone you come in contact with. Operating from your passion, power and purpose is the whole secret to life. If you're not working from that then you're missing what you're really here to do, especially if you want to help others."

"So passion plus power plus purpose equals change?"

"Yep."

"Ok, well I guess that is simple enough. But, here's where it's not easy for me. How do you know what each is?"

It was obvious Jake was waiting for this question. It's the question he gets asked all of the time.

"Passion is the fuel and desire that will get you through anything. What are you passionate about?" Jake asked Jim.

Here it came again. All of these questions Jim didn't know how to answer, so he fell silent. The creator of his own movie fell silent. Jake wanted to make it easy for him. "What do you love to do?"

"Capture people being real. I love interacting with them and learning."

"Good!" Jake was getting more energized by Jim's confession. "What's your vision?"

"You know maybe it's having people relate to what I'm doing and give them the courage to make a change in their own lives."

"Awesome! And do you believe you will?" Jake asked.

Jim was quiet. "I... I don't know yet."

CHAPTER 8

"You need that power."

"How do I get that?" Jim asked with doubt again.

"Go beyond your past mistakes. Think about the choices you are making now. Make other people's lives better and you will start to feel the power. You will feel it to the point that you don't even recognize the word "impossible."

Jim was starting to really dig this guy and he liked the idea of feeling powerful. "And purpose?" Jim was ready for the third power.

"You have a purpose. You're doing it now. You know why you're doing this. Most people don't have a purpose. You do. You're focusing on it."

"You're the first person who recognized that." Jim felt a new sense of self-knowing that he did actually have a purpose here and that for once in his life he was focused on something he believed in.

"You're going to make the shift you want. You already are. I can see it. With yourself and with the world, you are making that change. I guarantee you will inspire others to make changes. Keep at it Jim and… I didn't get your name behind the camera."

"Taz." Taz reached out his hand from behind and shook Jake's hand. "And he will. I know he will."

"As will you," Jake added.

"Thanks," Taz accepted.

Chapter 9

TO MOVE UP,
YOU'VE GOT TO MOVE DOWN

"Hey man, what's up?" Taz walked into the living room to find Jim slouched on the couch with the remote in his hand and a grumpy look on his face.

"I'm watching all these documentaries and they are so powerful. I was getting pumped up and then I realize that at the end of most of these, they are working for some sort of cause. They are doing something that will help a charity or organization or create a movement. Are we going to do that? I mean who are we helping on a bigger scale? What if this thing takes off and brings in a lot of attention? What can we do with the attention and the money that will help someone?" Jim was genuinely concerned about this and Taz could see it.

"I can tell you one thing," he sat next to Jim. "You're thinking right. That's what we need to do. Remember Jake said something about doing things for others and helping them? That's how we get power, by helping others." He stopped for a moment and thought. "Hey, I think I've got a guy we can talk to."

Three hours later, Jim, Taz and a tall guy named Richard Muscio were sitting at a coffee shop.

"So, you were actually blind?!" Jim couldn't believe his ears when he heard about this fantastically healthy looking guy, who was looking him straight in the eye telling him that he had lost sight in one eye when his daughter accidentally kicked him and had an ongoing series of retinal detachments in the other. He was blind.

"Yep, couldn't see a thing. I couldn't work or play tennis or do any of the things I loved to do except eat. I ended up gaining about 50 pounds." Jim looked at Richard now and could see that he clearly took it off.

"How'd you lose it? What'd you do?"

Taz smiled. He already knew the answer. He knew Richard through some philanthropic work.

"Well, I started to get some vision back in my right eye. But, it wasn't enough to return to my job or play tennis. So, my doc said I should start jogging. I laughed at him. There wasn't anything in me that said it wanted to run. Just the thought of it made me want to lay on the couch and eat! But, I did it anyway because at that time I didn't have anything else pushing me. So I started to walk 5 minutes, jog 5 minutes. I kept going. Next thing I know I'm down half the weight I gained. The doc took me off all of my meds. So, I kept going.

CHAPTER 9

Turns out, I was in my 40s before I discovered something I was really good at and it took losing my sight to get it. I became an endurance athlete. I've won 20 medals in my age group. While everyone else around me was having a midlife crisis, I was running! I felt great. So great that I decided to do more with it."

"What do you mean?" Jim asked.

"Well, it made me think. I could have gone down a bad path because something happened to me. Just like it does with everyone. Life happens. You can either make your life better or get sucked down. I started to realize that this is what was happening with teens. Their home life isn't good or they're having a rough time at school and they start getting into more trouble. They're eating bad, drinking, smoking, getting pregnant. They're missing out on life and they needed options. They just needed something to do before and after school to keep them out of these situations."

"Right, right." Jim was getting more intrigued by the minute.

"I got my community to share my cause and we created a series of races for these kids to get them moving. The money from the races goes to help these kids spend their time effectively."

"And that makes you feel great I bet."

"I feel great when I run and I feel great when I give. It's a win-win. It's about participating more than it is writing a check, you know?"

"I do." Jim took in the moment. "You know, Richard, I'll be honest, I thought to myself that I could take some of the money we make from this movie and I could donate it, but after hearing you, I want to participate in something. But, I don't know what."

"Do what means something to you." Richard said.

"I think I know what some of that is, but I'm still trying to figure out the bigger purpose." Jim could feel that discomfort again.

"Close your eyes." Richard said.

"What?"

"Yeah. Close your eyes. You're going to be blind for about five minutes here."

Jim looked at Taz with a little fright.

"Go on. Close 'em." Richard insisted. "Sometimes to move up, you've got to move down."

Jim finally closed his eyes feeling extremely uneasy. He didn't know what was going on and he couldn't see anything.

Thirty seconds went by and he was starting to go crazy. "Do I just keep them closed?"

"Keep 'em closed." Richard waited another thirty seconds. "Now, just imagine that this is your life now. You can't see and you can't change the fact that you can't see."

Jim's heart started to race and his palms were getting sweaty.

"Don't you open them. Keep them closed." Richard was very firm on this.

"Ok," Jim's voice was starting to shake. He hated this feeling.

Richard waited a few minutes this time before he said anything. "Now, what would you do differently if you could see again?"

Jim's mind started racing with images of lakes, boats, mountains, building houses for children, creating documentaries around the world. He saw himself being more daring and courageous than ever. It was as if he saw everything in this big bowl and he could have it. "I see so much." He was speechless when it came time to answer Richard, but Richard knew what that meant.

"Guess what?"

"What?" Jim replied.

"You can see. Now go do those things."

Jim opened his eyes.

Chapter 10

LOOK AROUND

The bookstore seemed filled with a lot of hopefuls. Jim recognized that trait in each and every person perusing the aisles. To his right was a woman who was squinting as she flipped through an art book.

To his left was a man with long hair, searching through an Egyptian history book. Just next to him was Taz looking at a documentary film book and admiring the old cameras. "So far, it looks awesome. Another month or so of interviews, edits and music." He shook his head, paused his page turning and looked at Jim, "We're going to have something good here Jim."

Jim was still watching the others and barely agreed with a, "mmm, hmm."

Taz just brushed him off. "I'm going to get a coffee. You want one?"

Jim now seemed to be entranced by one person who was sitting in one of the chairs with a book in front of him. The man wasn't reading and instead people watching, much like Jim. But, there was something about this man that captivated Jim. His subtle smile and calm disposition intrigued him. The man appeared totally uninfluenced by his surroundings, whereas other people looked desperate to find something because of everything around them. Jim was so lost that he forgot to respond to Taz. By the time he turned to answer him, Taz was already in line at the coffee kiosk in the mega bookstore.

He went back to the man sitting in the chair, who had one leg rested above the other. He wore glasses and dressed very casual, projecting a comfortable presence. Jim questioned for a moment if it would be odd to ask a total stranger why he seemed so peaceful and calm. A voice in his head, told him that, 'yes', it would be strange. Vowing to embrace uncomfortable situations and test his unnatural impulses, he decided to ask.

"Pardon me," Jim said as he walked up to the man. The man just smiled and widened his eyes. "I'm sorry to bother you."

"Not at all," The man replied.

"My name is Jim."

"Hello Jim, I'm Forrest."

"Forrest," Jim repeated with a smile. It matched.

"This will seem mighty strange for me to tell you, but I've been watching you for a moment."

"I know."

"You know?" Jim asked.

"Why, yes. You weren't very far from me and I could see you," he laughed softly.

"Yeah, I can see you are very aware, but also not distracted. It's an interesting combination and one that, frankly, I'm not familiar with. Are you always like this?"

"I might not always have been this way, but yes, for the most part I am. I'm just present."

"Right. I hear how important it is to be present, but I don't quite understand it or really know how to do it," Jim was embarrassed at his own confession, but hopeful at the same time that he would receive an answer.

Forrest closed his eyes for a moment and said nothing. Jim just watched him, wondering what was going on and if he might have made a mistake approaching this man who was just enjoying his time at the bookstore. But before he could think further, Forrest said, "Look around."

"Excuse me," Jim said.

With his eyes still closed, Forrest repeated himself, "Look around."

"So?" Jim looked around the bookstore.

"Take notice of everything you see."

Jim started to look at each book. He noticed the designs, the colors, the words and he noticed the people again looking at them.

Forrest opened his eyes. "You've been looking at the people around you and then you spotted me. You were present in that moment. You were asking for something and when you looked around you were able to find what you needed." Jim paused for a moment to let Forrest's words sink in. "When you need an answer," Forrest continued, "look around and bring yourself into the moment and what you need, will show up." Forrest gently smiled and looked down at his book again.

"Wow. That's so simple." Jim wasn't even quite sure what he was looking for, but this man struck his curiosity and answered a question he didn't even know he had. "How did you know that's what I needed to hear?"

Forrest looked up again. "When someone comes to me, I respond to them as if they were my child. That way I always know I'm giving the best answer filled with authenticity."

It warmed Jim's heart to know that there were people in the world like Forrest, who so selflessly gave. It brought a wave of calm within Jim and a sense of inner peace that he hadn't yet felt along this journey.

As Jim headed back to meet Taz, he noticed Taz had the camera perched up on his shoulder aimed at Jim. "Whatcha' recording?" Jim asked Taz as he approached.

"You." Taz responded.

"But, you're so far. How could you get anything?" Jim was confused.

"Doesn't matter. Trust me, I got something. Even from over here."

Chapter 11

A LESSON IN THE WAY

"I understand completely, I'm just not able to make a payment today. I'm out of work and I haven't been approved yet for unemployment. I'm actively looking and once I can, I will make that payment." Jim was just ending a troublesome phone call when Taz walked into the kitchen one early Friday morning.

"Should I even ask?" Taz wondered as he poured himself a bowl of cereal and took a sip of coffee.

"Ah, man. It's not your problem." Jim was feeling defeated right now. While one part of his life was beginning to feel fulfilled, another part was feeling completely unmanageable.

"Hey, you're my partner. If you have a problem, it's my problem too. We're a team, right?" Taz was encouraging, but Jim wasn't really biting.

"I'm running low on the cash I saved and I've got some payments to make and I just can't swing it right now," Jim confessed.

"Do you need some help? I mean what are you talking about here? A few hundred? We might have some in savings we could lend you."

"No, I can't do that to you. It's about time I found a job."

Taz laughed at his words, "You just said you were actively looking on the phone."

"Ah, I know."

"So, are you?"

"Well, no. I've been treating the film as my full time job," Jim admitted.

"Look, I'm happy to loan you some money, but Em and I don't have a lot as you know and we both work hard to keep things afloat. We love that you're here and I love that we're creating this film, but don't feel bad if you have to do something on the side to compensate."

Jim felt riddled with guilt now. He had hoped it would move along faster and that the stay with Taz be temporary. But, reality hit him hard with no income and no confidence regarding a hand out for his situation. "Yeah, you're right. I've just been putting so much time into this."

"Look, we're still doing this either way. So we both put in extra time on the weekends now. We'll do some nights too. That's what this is about."

"What kind of work am I going to do? I mean same old stuff. I don't even know if they'll give me a referral now."

Just then Emily walked in the room with another woman. "Hey guys!" She looked at both of the men who were deep in conversation. "Um, am I interrupting something here?"

"Jim needs some work." Taz blurted out.

Jim was not so appreciative of the announcement in front of the beautiful woman that Emily stood next to.

"Oh, ok." Emily said. "By the way, this is my friend Clarissa. Clarissa Burt.

They all greeted each other. Clarissa asked immediately after, "What sort of work are you looking for?"

"Writing. Film. That sort of thing," Taz spoke for Jim.

"Well, I just left another job for a paper back in Philly. We're making a documentary out here and, well..." Jim was stumbling over his own words and feeling embarrassed.

"I get it," Clarissa bounced back with. She knew exactly what he was feeling. "You got a little something in your way right now?"

Jim tilted his head in question.

"Life put a little something in your way. You want to make this movie, but you need to take care of business at the same time, right?" She clarified.

"Yeah. I guess so." Suddenly Jim seemed brighter because someone understood him.

"It's ok. It's just a lesson. It's not even a setback. A lesson pushes you forward. Lessons will always get in the way, but if they didn't, we couldn't move up."

Jim took a deep breath. "I like that perspective. I never thought of it that way."

"I know about lessons, trust me. I know what it's like to have everything and not have anything. Just make sure you appreciate what you have and know that you deserve it then the lessons that get in the way are that much more easily learned."

"I just feel like things are always changing and once I get good with something, another thing pops up."

"Oh, yeah. I know that too. You're lucky."

"Really? Lucky?" Jim wasn't so sure.

"Look, the only constant in life is change. The more you recognize the changes, the more you are learning. Life will always put things in your way so that you can learn. If you don't learn the lesson, it will throw more at you. Learn the lesson and move on. When something else comes up, learn from it and keep going. One day you will look back and be grateful for all that life put in your way. One day you will have that film that people care about. Documentaries impact people because they're real life, right?" Clarissa asked with a point in mind.

"Well... yeah." Jim was hesitant.

"So be real, Jim. Show them what you have to do to make this happen. Sometimes it's finding a job along the way to support the dream. Let people see what life really is and how they can make something big happen even when they have

Chapter 11

a job." Clarissa smiled after she was finished and looked over at Emily to give her the nod that she was ready to go.

Jim's mood shifted, almost instantaneously. She was right. Here he was feeling embarrassed about his situation, when in reality, it could be the very thing that would make people relate even more. After all, this was a film about real people on their real rise.

Chapter 12

THE BEST SHOTS

"I know it's not glamorous, but at least it's something. And remember it's only temporary," Taz told Jim as he walked him through the halls of the studio he worked at. One of the producers had just fired an assistant and while it wasn't something Jim was used to doing and felt way overqualified for, he thought for now, it would be a good choice to take the position as the new production assistant.

"I don't even drink coffee, so I don't know how good I'll be at making it. I'm also not even good at running my own errands. I barely know the city either." Jim was searching for every excuse of why this job wasn't right for him.

Taz stopped him in the middle of the hallway just feet before the producer's door. "Hey!" He said it loud. Two people passing turned to look back. "You have a job now Jim. Stop telling me what you're not good at and think about the things you *are* good at. Remember Tara?" Taz asked.

Jim thought for a moment and then laughed, "Yeah, Tara."

Last week when Jim and Taz were shooting footage of children playing, for the opening of the documentary, a woman at the park came up to them and asked what they were doing.

"Oh we're creating a documentary. We've got an opening narrative piece and thanks to these parents we can use their children. These kids are a perfect shot." Taz took a break to put in more film for the camera.

"Can I ask a question?" The woman said as they fiddled with their equipment.

"Sure," Jim answered.

"How do you get your best shots?"

"Well, a lot of times we see something that captivates us. We know how we see it and then we focus with the camera and that's when it happens."

"Interesting, kind of like life I guess."

"Yeah? How so?" Jim was just about finished cleaning the lens for Taz.

"Well, if you look for the greatness, dial into the vision and get the right focus, the clearer it becomes."

Taz and Jim looked at each other right away.

"Next shot!" They both called out right away.

"Can you say that again?" Jim asked. "On camera?"

The woman started laughing. "Sure, I guess. But, what's this for again?"

"Oh, it's a documentary about how people go about achieving greatness."

Chapter 12

She nodded, "I get it."

"Get it?" Jim confirmed.

"Well, what do you want me to do?"

"Exactly what you just did." Jim said.

Remaining somewhat caught off guard, the woman went with it.

"And we're rolling," Taz gave them very little warning. Jim was ready to go.

"We just met this woman… what was your name?" Jim spoke to the camera and her at the same time.

"Tara."

"Great. Tara! Hi, Tara."

"Hi," Tara said still a little unsure of what was happening.

"How does one get their best shot at life?" Jim put the pressure on Tara to deliver. She wiped her blonde hair from her eyes and looked at Jim. The camera was directly on her as she looked to Jim, just off camera now.

"Dial in to the vision, look for greatness. There's something great in everything that you do. If you focus, you will see the gifts, the alliances and the opportunities. There's possibility everywhere. Don't let fear bring out the negative or it will cripple the dream. Just be aware and focus."

Taz zoomed in on Tara. The image appeared hazy at first and with each word he focused more and more, until a beautiful frame on Tara's last words became crystal clear.

"Remember what she said?" Taz reminded Jim in the hallway. "This is an opportunity to make new alliances. Look for the gifts in this. There's plenty of people here who can help us. Let's stay focused and use this opportunity to make the possibility clear."

Jim took a deep breath. "Ok, let's do it." He walked into the producer's door. "Hello Mr. Burgess, I'm Jim MacDonald, your new P.A." Taz captured Jim from behind on camera.

Chapter 13

CONSTANT REMINDERS

Jim came home after what he considered a grueling day at work. His clothes were stained with soup that he spilled on himself after trying to juggle three lunches, three coffees and camera all at once. His skills as a personal assistant lacked but he steadfastly worked on mastering them. He tried to capture as much of the experience as he could. If Taz wasn't busy, he used him as an opportunity to document his destructive clumsiness. Jim now faced high demands at the studio. The producer he worked for required him to assist multiple directors at once. He fetched and delivered from building to building non-stop all day long. He was exhausted by the end of the day and had to remind himself this was all part of his own rise, as challenging as it was proving to be.

"See your results and celebrate your achievements," a voice popped into his head. It was Flor. Flor Mazeda was a friend of Julia's. He remembered one night when he was upstairs with Julia and Nathan after Nathan had a birthday party. Everyone had left and Flor remained there with her children. Nathan was having a difficult time at school that week and Flor was offering advice.

"Always remind him of what he's done and what he has achieved. Maybe it's a picture the teacher hung up on the wall. Maybe he did a great job sharing with his class and the teacher gave him a special note for it. Whatever it is, he should be reminded of it. Those are the things that make us feel good. When we forget those things, we forget how wonderful we really are."

Jim looked back and remembered Flor's words and how they applied to this situation. Struggling with a job that he felt overqualified for was taking his thoughts away from whom he really was. He was focused on all of the things he couldn't do.

"When you remember and celebrate what you are good at, you can become better at the other things." Flor told Julia. Jim listened that night and somehow it stayed with him.

Tonight he planned to go to bed early and think of all the things he had accomplished up until this point. It didn't matter how large or small; it was the feeling associated with them that brought him comfort and good pride.

As he started to think of the strides he made, he also thought of the advances to come. He closed his eyes and saw his film. He imagined the filming of it and the people that it would touch. He could see the premiere of his film and the people in his life that came to see it. His mother and father would be there and he would finally feel a sense of accomplishment in their eyes.

His friends from college who gave up on his dream when he did would praise his talents and ability to make it happen. He would inspire old classmates who also gave up and urge them to pick up their dreams. The feeling of self-worth filled his body as he imagined the impact he could have with this film.

The next day he delivered coffees without anyone asking and he had scripts printed and ready to go an hour before call time. He had a new attitude based on the celebration of his own self. Holding the camera in his own face, while waiting for his next task he said, "This just might work."

Chapter 14

REMEMBER WHO YOU ARE

Friday's production shut down early and Jim didn't need to stay for the entire day. He was almost two weeks into his new job and he was feeling pretty positive for the most part. He tried to chime in on conversations with staff, set designers, actors, anchors and essentially anyone who would offer him anything. But, for the most part, he was shut down. He figured it was too early on for anyone to care much about him and the fact that he was a PA, didn't give him much clout. He said as much to his future audience, this early afternoon while sitting on a bench in the studio lobby with the camera held on his lap.

"If I were in their position, I might not talk to myself either. After all, what can a guy like me who's a PA at my age, offer them? Most of them are high on their rise. I'm still at the starting point. What could I offer them?"

"Remember who you are." A man's voice casually said as doors opened.

Feeling interrupted, Jim looked up and gave the man an unfriendly look.

"Sorry, the echo is louder when everyone's gone." The man apologized. "If you know who you are, you know what you have to offer. It doesn't matter where you are at."

Jim was now interested. He kept the camera rolling so that he was being filmed and the man's voice was being heard.

"I'm Joshua. Joshua Phair. Just got done shooting a segment for the A.M. news slot. What are you doing out here?"

Jim pointed to the camera, "It's for a documentary." Jim didn't explain, he went right to the bait that hooked him, "So, tell me. How does one *know* themselves?"

"My dad always told me before I left the house, 'Remember who you are, son.' See, you are more than what you are right now, but you may not believe it. Well, I know you don't from what I heard. You're in doubt of your own greatness."

The camera caught Jim's vulnerability. It couldn't have been captured better. From underneath, the audience would see his eyes that would reflect the truth in Joshua's words. He had no words, he just nodded.

Joshua continued, "Take away all of your roles and everything that you have to do and what's left?"

Jim stayed silent as he questioned what was left.

"Well?" Joshua wasn't settling for the silence.

Jim lifted his head a bit. "I guess I'm just a guy trying to make something of myself."

"Before that."

"Before that?" Jim repeated.

"Yeah, who were you before being someone trying to make something of yourself?" Joshua clarified.

"I was a guy with a job trying to do it good enough."

"No. Before that."

"A guy in college wanting to make films for people that would inspire them."

"Before that."

Jim was searching.

"Before the stuff, who are you?"

"I'm Jim."

"You're Jim." Joshua nodded.

In that moment, both Jim and Joshua knew what that meant. Jim was compassion. He was heart. He was enthusiasm. He was life.

"Always remember who you are." Joshua repeated.

Jim stopped the camera from rolling.

Chapter 15

YOU'RE DIFFERENT NOW

Taz and Jim sat at the studio cafeteria for lunch. Taz took a bite of his sandwich and asked with a full mouth, "Things getting better with the job?"

"It's going good." Jim said as he buttered bread.

"That piece with Joshua? Killer. It's really incredible."

"I've been thinking about it since. I know." Jim agreed.

They both sat quiet for a few moments. Taz ate his lunch and Jim seemed to be buttering his bread far longer than was needed.

"You sure all is good? Or do you just need that much butter?"

Jim shook his head and put down the butter knife and bread. "I don't know man. You know I feel really good about everything. I feel more confident each day. But, the more we get and the better we do, I can't help but think what if and what a waste."

Taz swallowed hard. "What do you mean?"

"I mean what if we kept going in college? Where would we be now? We're surrounded every day by these magnificent people who have accomplished so much. If we are moving this fast on a documentary, what could we have done if we didn't quit? I mean did we just waste all of these years?"

A man sitting at a table right next to them turned to them. "Pardon the interruption, but you're looking at things all wrong."

Taz nodded his head in agreement and then stopped and said, "Wait, are we though? Maybe he's right. Maybe we did waste all of these years."

"Well, I have no clue what you wasted and what you are talking about, but I can tell you this, whatever it is, you won't go far beating yourself up about it." He pointed to the empty chair at Taz and Jim's table. "Do you mind?"

"Come on over!" Taz said.

The man set his tray down. "I'm Richard by the way. Richard Barrier."

"Oh right. I saw you on set for an interview about a phone app that solves the problem from distracted driving and texting while driving."

"Right." Richard smiled.

"Here's the thing. Who you are now and who you are back then are totally different." He looked at Jim. "Did I hear you say you've accomplished so much so fast in a short period of time?"

Jim nodded. "Well, yeah."

"Did you do that back then?"

"No."

"Because you're different now."

"You sure are," Taz agreed.

"So why get upset about something you didn't do back then, but would do now? Why get upset about something you did do back then and wouldn't do now?" Richard said.

"You're right." Jim said.

"You've come far. If you can move quickly now and get results faster now, it's because you are a better person. You are learning and growing. Look back and take pride in who you are becoming. Let that be your driving force."

Jim nodded and finally took a bite of his buttered bread.

Chapter 16

BODY ARMOR

"I just don't think people are going to care. But, I'm sure it will be a nice project for you to have under your belt. I'm sorry. I just don't want to be a part of it. It seems very amateurish and pointless." Charles Miller, executive producer of *Coffee with Rori*, a morning talk show, told Jim. Jim had just asked if Charles would be filmed for the documentary. His response was like a hand entering his guts and twisting them. He whipped out his phone to text Taz the disheartening news.

"Don't let it get to you." A man said coming up from behind Jim.

"Misha, hey." Jim replied. "I know, it's not easy to deal with a 'no'."

Misha Elias was visiting his wife, Stacey, who was doing a series of fitness spots on one of the shows. He'd been there for the past week and would talk to Jim on the side during taping.

"If someone says 'no' to you, just brush it off." Misha said.

"Easy to say, not so easy to do." Jim admitted. He was feeling really low.

"Look back when I lived in Mexico, my dream was to come to the United States, but my friends told me that I couldn't do it and that I wouldn't make it. But, I'm here, right?"

"Right" Jim replied.

"And even when I arrived in the United States, people would still tell me that I would not be successful. But, I never gave up." Misha continued. "As you can see, I have gone through much rejection in my life and also in my business. And that is when I learned that I needed to create my own body armor. So, the trick is that when I get attacked or in this case, you get attacked, your armor has to be thick enough so that the negative comments and criticism don't get to you." Misha told him.

"I like that Misha." Jim said excitedly.

"What is happening to you now, happens in every industry and especially the creative one. This is why you need to create your own body armor."

"But, what is body armor?" Jim asked.

"Body armor is your mental and emotional strength; it's the ability to control your thoughts, fears, and feelings when you get attacked by negative comments. Your body armor has to be so strong that nothing can penetrate it. It has to be built with the strength of your goals and dreams," Misha replied.

Chapter 16

"That is so powerful, Misha. I never thought of it that way, but it still bothers me, you know?" Jim said.

"Oh, I know." Misha replied. "But, you can't let other people's opinions or negativity affect you personally. It has nothing to do with you as a person. Just let the negativity bounce off of your armor and you'll see the opportunity in the situation."

"Yeah, I should film the rejection. I mean that's part of the rise right?"

"Sure is. And remember, as long as you are wearing your body armor, rejection just makes you stronger and it should be the fuel to push you to accomplish more in life. Keep going; don't give up at the first sign of a struggle. When you get a "no," don't stop there. Keep going!" Misha said.

Later on, Jim went back to Charlie's office and requested a replay of what he had said earlier. He rudely declined. Taz caught the voice. He will remain nameless in the film.

Chapter 17

BEHIND THE STAGE

Jim finished work for the day and decided to meet Taz over at his side of the studio. He walked over to the red recording lights and waited. He sent Taz a text to let him know he was waiting outside. When the lights went off, Taz came to the door and let Jim in.

Jim loved hanging out at the show Taz worked on, which was filmed for the prime time shows at night. "You gotta see this woman. You'll dig what she has to say." Taz rushed Jim over to a good viewing area where he wouldn't be seen.

Five minutes later and they were rolling again. A chic woman with short blonde hair and an Australian accent began speaking to the host of the show.

"We've all had those moments where things just don't seem to be going your way. You start to question everything you've been doing and why. And even more, you doubt yourself. That's when things get dangerous because you are telling your mind to believe all of these... lies."

"Lies?" the classy dark-haired woman hosting the show asked.

"Oh yes. They are all lies. All of the negative mumblings that goes on in your mind are lies. Yet we believe them, so we act from them."

"I know there's more to this than you have time to share, but what's the short version?"

The Australian woman looked relaxed and happy as she spoke. It was hard for Jim not to smile watching her. "If we have the power to make ourselves believe the lies, why not believe the truth, which is, you have a genius mind that is capable of achieving anything you want it to."

"And you do this yourself with this incredible technology?"

"I do."

Music started to fade in.

"For more information on how you can train your brain to achieve anything, please visit our site," she turned to her guest. "And a special thank you to Natalie Ledwell for joining us this evening." She turned back to the camera. "And thank you, our fans, for watching."

As the show closed and off set noises could resume, Taz ran over to Jim. "Cool, right?"

"What's this technology about?"

"Ah man, it's cool. You can create your own movie about what you want in life. You keep watching it over and over and your brain is programmed to make you make it happen."

Chapter 17

"Where can I get it?" Jim was eager.

"I already got it. We can start tonight." Taz was pumped. "Even better, I'm going to introduce you. I've already been telling her on the breaks about what we're doing. Producers gave us rights to use her clip in the movie. What do you think?"

Jim could only smile.

"Natalie!" Taz called her over.

"Ah, hi, you must be Jim!" she seemed genuinely excited and Jim couldn't help but smile.

"I loved watching you. Thank you for your information."

"Well, I think it's a really great thing you both are doing and I'm so happy that I will get to play a part in it." She said with sincerity.

She had no idea what an impact she would make, Jim thought to himself.

Later that evening Taz and Jim made a three minute film showcasing the success and impact this film would have and vowed to watch it two times a day.

Chapter 18

THE PYRAMID

"I have an idea." Jim said as he stood on line at a busy coffee shop.

"You're going to try coffee and we're going to get it on film?" Taz retorted.

"No, and not funny. We're going to ask people to pull three things out of their pocket and film them."

"I don't get it." Taz was lost.

"Well, I'm not finished yet." Jim was getting excited.

"Ok, explain because I can't imagine seeing crumpled up receipts or change is going to influence anyone deeply."

Jim threw Taz a look displaying his irritation. "Three things that they can pull out and tell us off the fly what matters and why? Three reasons to climb to the top. Three things that keep you going when you feel knocked down. Three things you can do right now to change your life. Then we'll take it all and piece it together for a montage." He waited. "Are you seeing where I'm going with this?"

Taz looked at Jim wanting so bad to make a joke, but he couldn't. "I love it. Let's go." He started to take out the camera.

"Ready? Here? Now? Let's get her." Jim said quietly saying to the person next in line to order.

"You mean this lady standing right in front of us?" Taz asked.

Jim tapped the woman lightly on the shoulder, who was on her phone. She turned around and offered a big bright smile and a finger to indicating them to hold for a moment. Jim nodded in acceptance.

"It sounds beautiful. I'll call you soon to follow up." The woman finished her conversation and returned her attention to Jim and Taz. "Yes?"

"We're making a movie. We're collecting the three pieces of wisdom from each person we can get. Would you mind if we filmed you and your three things?"

She laughed right away. "Oh I can tell you three things right now. They are the three things I live by." The guys looked at each other both acknowledging how incredible and fun this small segment of the film could be.

"Well, we have some topics..."

"Oh, I don't need a topic. This applies to everything no matter what. Are you rolling?" She was anxious to share what she had.

"Give me just a sec." Taz said as he started the camera.

"Well go ahead and order your drink."

CHAPTER 18

"Can't we have the barista in the background? I like the idea of her taking a moment in between ordering to tell us." Taz commented.

Jim looked at the woman for approval. "That alright with you?"

"It's great!"

Jim detected an accent in her voice. "What's your name?"

"I'm Sonja Sbitani." She was so bright and uplifting. It was almost odd to Taz and Jim that she was so willing to do this.

"Alright we're good!" Taz gave them the cue and they were off.

"Oh ready?" She asked. Taz threw her a finger that signified she could start speaking and so she did. "Life is actually very simple. If you follow these three steps, you cannot help but succeed. Ready?" Taz and Jim nodded off camera. The barista stood smiling in the background. "One, help each other and love unconditionally! Our real purpose is to learn how to unite our world by helping one another and to love unconditionally. Two, be completely honest with yourself – is everything that you are doing for the good of everyone? By taking ourselves out of the equation and not asking, 'What's in it for me?' but rather genuinely working for the good of everyone, we personally prosper, since we're part of the greater good. Three, live from complete truth. This is most important because it is imperative that we always operate from the core of our being, which is truth.

This is done through our thoughts, communication and our actions. If you follow those three basic truths, your life will manifest in ways you never thought possible."

"So adorable you are!" Taz said. He practically wanted to take her with them. But, they had more shooting to do.

"Can I hug you?" Jim asked.

"Of course!" She hugged both of them. They treated her to her cappuccino and said their goodbyes.

The rest of the people that day were not as easy, but they did get a few more that were willing. At the end of the day, they had a good collection of messages that would translate well onto film. As the days went on and the cast came together, Taz' and Jim's enthusiasm reached an all-time high.

Chapter 19

WHAT KEEPS YOU UP AT NIGHT?

"This guy was good." Jim said as he watched back the replay of the day and all of the messages people brought in. He rewound the tape and watched Jonny Carter. He could see it perfectly now. The montage would have each person stating just one of their three nuggets. It would flash to each person, in and out, in and out. It was a fantastic stream of momentum with varying people. It covered all walks of life and what they held important. Jim didn't care if he agreed or not; the point was to show what was important to them and to take something from it as he hoped his audience members would. But, there was one guy in the mix after the montage that stopped Jim. The montage would end on Jonny. Jim watched again and took notes.

"Give us your three?" Taz' voice in the background said as the camera zoomed in on Jonny's face. Sounds of honking horns and people chatting behind them resonated loudly. But, even with the tall buildings and city life happening in full force, Jonny remained very calm during the focused shot.

"I have just one," he said. "What keeps you up at night?"

The camera went in closer on his face, leaving the city behind a blur.

"It's a double edged sword. Are you so excited about something that you can't stop thinking about it? Or are you so miserable that you can't stop thinking about it?" These are the areas of your life that you need to focus on, no matter how difficult they are to face. Anything you do that is not answering those burning questions is a distraction that is not serving you. And sometimes, meeting those questions means redefining your self. Jonny looked behind him at the bustle and then back to the camera. "How do you find your passion amongst all of this? How do you differentiate between growing the bank account and doing what you love? I had the big account, but I didn't have the big life. Every night, I stayed awake thinking about the one thing I really wanted to do and I thought about how sad it was that I wasn't doing it. The answer was right there. So, I did it." He paused for a moment and Taz got a closer shot. "What keeps *you* up at night?"

"And fade out." Taz said standing just behind Jim.

Jim looked behind him to notice Taz. "It's good, right?"

"I know what keeps you up." Taz smiled at Jim and tapped his shoulder and left the room.

Chapter 20

FRAME BY FRAME

"I think I've got most of this edited as a rough go. I just want to see it as we go along you know?" Jim was talking fast and Taz couldn't keep up. "I just can't seem to get all of these people that I want scheduled fast enough. I'm trying to find the right people and book them so we can make this deadline that we have. We also need to start making the right connections so we have someone to show this to. And have you gotten more film? I also think we need to get a new boom. The sound is starting to get scratch."

"Woa! Relax." Taz shouted.

Jim stopped with eyes wide open. He was shocked that Taz yelled out. He never yells out.

"You're trying to do everything."

"Well, how else is it going to get done."

"By getting help."

"From who? We can't afford help."

Just then Jim's phone started making a funny robot noise. It was a text message.

"Do you remember Deborah?" Jim asked Taz breaking the uncomfortable moment.

"From back in the day?" Taz squinted his eyes.

"Yeah."

"Deb?" Taz said.

"Yes! Deb." Jim laughed.

"I loved that girl!" Taz was getting excited thinking about her.

"I know and I asked her to come meet us. We're going to film her. I follow her online and she's always got these incredible messages. So, at first I thought we fly to the west coast, meet her and meet more people. Then I realized that we didn't really have a lot of money to do that."

Taz laughed in agreement. "So, she's coming all this way?"

"Well, it just so happens when I emailed her, she was going to be on the east coast for business. So, we've got her today at 4pm."

"Ha! I can't wait to see her again." Taz, Deborah and Jim had lots of good times together and it was going to be fun to reunite.

After a few screams and hugs, the party of three let the hostess take them to their table. "Wow, you guys haven't changed too much." Deborah said with a huge grin on her face.

CHAPTER 20

"Deborah Ives Lillywhite, you look amazing. You *have* changed. You look very bright and happy. What's going on?" Jim asked.

"Ah," she paused and took in the moment. "Everything happened and everything is happening. I'm just so happy." She had an undeniable look of fulfillment on her face.

"So, can we film right now?"

"Now?" She asked. "Can we eat first?"

"Can't. Something's happening now and I want to get it. More raw that way." Jim said with urgency.

Taz whipped out the camera and prepped everything.

"So noise, all of that doesn't matter?"

"It's a documentary, Deb. Right? We want the raw footage."

"Right. Gosh I'm so happy you guys are doing this again. Wow."

Once Taz was set up, they were ready to go."

"I'm excited!" Deb was as bubbly as ever and she was feeding off of their excitement.

"So, where have you been that can help us on where we're going?" Jim asked. Taz had a wide shot of the two of them sitting in a booth. He waited for Deborah's response, but there was silence. She smiled as the silence continued and Jim allowed for it. Taz finally realized something was happening and he got a closer shot of her eyes. They were filling up with tears. Her exuberance in that moment suddenly softened and she was brought to tears.

"I'm sorry," she finally said.

"Don't be," Jim said calmly. "Actually, we need these moments. I needed this moment." Taz zoomed in on Jim.

"I couldn't do everything and I tried to." She looked off beyond their space.

Jim nodded his head in agreement. "How do you get everything done then?"

"Accept the uncertainty," she said without a break.

"What do you mean?" Jim asked.

"You get so worked up on how everything has to go. Stay focused on the outcome. It doesn't matter how you get there, just that you do. If you try to control every step of the way and do everything yourself, it will be a struggle to get there. Isn't this about the rise?" She looked into his eyes.

"Well, yeah."

"Don't you want to enjoy it?"

"Yeah," he said softly.

"Don't miss out on the fun part because you are trying to do it all. The more you let others help, the more involved they get to be. The energy will change and you will feel a shift when you allow others in and let them help. Don't worry about how you can get help or how you are going to pay for it." She laughed and nodded her head. "You're worried about that, right?" Jim rolled his eyes. Guilty. "Just know the result will happen and take the help when it's offered. Sign up for mastermind groups or better yet, start your own. Help others and they will help you. It's been one of the

Chapter 20

most freeing beautiful experiences I've ever had – giving up control and letting others in. Accept the uncertainty and be open to whatever comes along to serve you and this project. Jim – take it frame by frame. I promise you will see the change. I did." Deborah pursed her lips and then smiled.

"Frame by frame," Jim repeated.

"Frame by frame takes you to scene by scene and upward." Deborah was soft in her words.

Just thinking about it in those terms relieved the pressure from Jim. From now on, he would accept help and he would offer it as well.

Chapter 21

THE PAY OFF

Jim and Taz met after work outside the studio building. Jim was jazzed. With the money he made, he was able to pay some bills and even contribute to Taz' household expenses. He had bought groceries for the family the night before and he did all of the laundry in the house. It felt good and today in return he felt as if a prayer was answered.

"Wait 'til you hear this!" Jim said practically jumping out of his pants.

"Tell me. I'm getting nervous just watching you."

"Good. Because the pressure is really on now. The stakes are high and we need to perform." Jim was talking fast again.

"Should I be scared?" Taz said.

"Maybe." Jim said as he brought Taz over to a nearby bench. "Sit down."

Taz sat down wearing caution on his face.

"I got us a showing at the independent film festival taking place on Broadway."

"Um, I know that one. I go every year. Jim, that's two months away."

"Yeah, I know. Can we do it?" He started shaking his head. "No. No. I mean we can do it, right? I mean… can we?"

Taz raised his eyebrow. "This is totally awesome," his voice didn't match excitement at all.

"Why don't you sound excited when you say that?"

"How on earth can we have this and marketing and everything done in two months?"

"Right. They need to have a finished copy in one month."

"Are you kidding me?" Taz jumped up. "Jim, what did you tell them?"

"Yes?" Jim's bubble was starting to burst.

"I think it's really great that somehow you peaked interest in our movie, but I know how these things work. They need to see a finished product. FINISHED product, Jim. We're not even close to a rough product." Taz was being realistic.

"But, I told them…" Jim started.

"Listen, maybe we can make it for next year. Maybe we need to focus on doing this right and not rushing into something we can't deliver. That will only hurt us. I mean I thought our goal was to have our own showing."

"So, what do I do? I told Jessica, the woman I spoke to and in charge of the film line up, that we had no problem

CHAPTER 21

delivering. I sort of made it sound like we were really close to being done."

Taz took a deep breath. "There's someone you need to talk to."

He took out his phone and activated his voice command, "Call Miranda Larson." Jim looked at him puzzled.

"Hi, it's Miranda," a cheerful voice answered the phone on the other end.

"Hey gorgeous, it's Taz."

"Taz! What the heck?! It's been forever! Uh oh. Are you in trouble?" Miranda joked.

"Actually…"

"Really? What's up?" She asked.

"I told you I was making that documentary, right? With my buddy Jim?"

"Yeah! And I haven't talked to you since you began. How's it going?" She had concern in her voice.

"Well, the filming is going great. Getting lots of great people. It's progressing quite nicely actually. Really good pace. As it should be…." He looked at Jim who accepted the look of punishment from Taz.

"Ok, I hear it in your voice. What did you do?"

"I did it!" Jim chimed in.

"Oh, Jim, Miranda. Miranda meet Jim." Taz made a phone introduction.

"Hi Jim."

"I sort of promised that we could have this ready in one month so we could be in the line-up at a film festival."

"But…." She leads him,

"There's no way." Taz said.

"I see." Miranda said.

"Miranda's really successful with her clients. She make deals happen and there's a reason people keep coming back to her," Taz explained to Jim. "Can you tell them why, Miranda?"

She laughed. "I don't like to get caught in a whirlpool of bull… well you know what."

"Ok…" Jim was waiting for more.

"There are a lot of times people want something to happen and they want it to happen right now. Sometimes my answer is, 'yes, I can make that happen' and sometimes no matter what the competitors promise they can do, I have to tell them when it's just not realistic. My clients always tell me that they may not like my answers all the time, but they love that I never lie. See Jim, if you overpromise you lose integrity with that person. Be certain that you can deliver before you make the promise."

"Crap." Jim said. He didn't think of it that way. "I was trying to be optimistic. I thought if I tell her I can, then the pressure is on and I have to do it. You know it's like declaring I will do it?"

"Oh I get it and I think that's awesome, but at the same time you have to be able to follow through first for yourself

Chapter 21

before you can for others. Having that integrity will always pay off even if it means a bit more of struggle. It's better to work hard and fulfill your promises then to work your butt off trying to make good on a promise and then not be able to turn it in." Miranda said. "Trust me, I know where you're at. I made it a point after too many bad experiences, that I would always be impeccable in my communication."

"What should I do now?" Jim felt a little beaten now that he made this error, but at the same time a little relieved.

"Go back to this person and apologize and tell her that it's important to you to deliver. You realized you don't have enough time to make this the film you want it to be. Jim, the world needs this film even if it's shown later. Be grateful you have this contact. She will probably respect you coming back and being honest and in the long run, you will have a meaningful relationship and admiration from this woman." Miranda was immaculate with her own words and Jim valued her advice.

"I'm going to do it." Jim looked over at Taz who seemed a lot calmer than he was a few minutes ago.

"So, can I come to the first showing?"

"Now, that I can say with 100% certainty – yes, you can!"

Chapter 22

LOOKING AHEAD

After a long phone call with Jessica, Jim felt liberated in a way. For a moment he thought he might have been missing a golden opportunity, but what he came to find was that in being loyal, he deepened a relationship that he could serve and that would serve him.

The drive to push forward was heightened now. Suddenly, even though the pressure to have a polished project was decreased, he felt a sense of panic again reaching the final vision. Why was he feeling so rushed? Was it that he didn't really think it could happen and he had to do it soon enough to prove it would?

He was standing outside a smoothie bar waiting for his order as all these thoughts came to him. Out of nowhere a ball, something hit his ankle. "Sorry!" a woman behind him said. She picked up the toy that hit him and handed it back to a little girl.

"That's ok." He looked at the little girl who was smiling and he couldn't help but smile back. "Hi there, what's your name?"

"This is Carly," The woman said.

"Hi Carly," Jim answered back. "She's really cute," he said to her mother.

"Yep, she's my inspiration every day."

This caught Jim's attention. While, he assumed every mother felt that way about their child, few often said it to a total stranger. It was that remark coupled with her endearing eyes towards her daughter that probed Jim to ask more.

"Without sounding ignorant, can I ask why?"

She giggled a bit at his words. "Of course you can ask. In fact, the more people I can share Carly's story with, the better."

"I wish I had my camera." Jim said under his breath.

"Sorry? Did you say camera?"

"Yeah, I'm making a documentary about people's journey in life and their rise to the top. We don't have much from children and it just dawned on me that they are on their own rise too."

"I'll tell you what, why don't you film me with your phone?"

Jim never thought of that. "Hmm. Yeah, it will look kind of rough, but we are going for that raw appeal and using whatever vessel of media we have, so... are you sure you don't mind?"

CHAPTER 22

"Will a lot of people see this?"

"You bet!" Jim was sure of that, especially now.

"Here we go!" She pulled her two-year-old daughter over in her stroller. "I'm Sandi Gugliotti and this is Carly," she said into the phone held camera.

"Carly is what I like to call, 'My Miracle Baby.' Every moment of her life so far has been filled with miracles. She was born with bilateral cleft lip and palate with low birth weight. I found out about this deformity when she was in my womb. At first, I felt immense fear about how she would look or how other people would perceive her. But I relied on science to alleviate my fears. I researched every aspect of her condition. Science always strips the emotions from a situation."

Sandi smiled and looked up to the left as though remembering a clear vision of what took place. When her focus on the camera returned, she took a deep breath and continued.

"Carly had her first surgery, which repaired the lip when she was 5 months old. When the doctor came out of the operating room, the first thing she said was, "Don't worry, but...!""

"That is never a good thing," Jim said.

"No, she had found a small white bump on the tip of Carly's nose that required multiple MRIs and CAT scans to identify."

Just then Carly let out a cry of impatience pointing to the toy she was playing with that had fallen on the ground. Sandi reached down to pick it up and handed it to her. Then she patted her on the head lovingly and continued speaking. "On Christmas eve of 2010, I received a call from a brain surgeon, who told me that the white bump, which had grown to the size of a dime, was a dermoid cyst and has grown a string up into her nose toward her brain. They had to remove it and close off the passage to the brain that it had created, or any fluid that made it through that canal could possible kill her."

Jim stopped her there with a look of shock on his face and said, "She obviously survived the surgery, right? I mean, she looks healthy and active."

With a smile of relief, Sandi replied, "Yes, yes, thank goodness. But, that was indeed the beginning of the rise. I spent the next thirty days donating blood and preparing for the surgery the best way I knew how. I avoided the emotions and focused on the science. I learned every aspect of her condition, the treatment, the recovery, the surgeons, etc..." She paused momentarily, taking in her surroundings. Then she looked right into the camera and said, "When I went to the hospital the day of surgery, I thought I was completely ready to take this on. But when I handed them my baby, something happened. As they walked through the door, taking Carly with them, I flipped out!"

Chapter 22

"I would, too!" Jim interjected, offering compassion and understanding.

"I ran as fast as I could out of the hospital, down the street, across the parking lot, at full speed. That was strange because at the time, I was unable to run due to a permanent knee injury. But that day, I ran." She reached down and touched her left knee as to show him that there was obvious scarring. "When I got to my car, I shut the door and let out a very loud scream. Then I took a deep breath again and let out a second scream. Time stopped, I heard silence, and then a strange vision appeared before my eyes. It was Carly. She was nineteen and she was beautiful. She had long dark hair and freckles, which as you can see she does not right now, but I do," she said pointing to Carly's clear skin. "As I looked upon her, she was staring out of a window, the way young girls do when they are daydreaming about a boy!" Sandi smiled in that moment with a calming expression that Jim wanted to be a part of.

She took a moment and then continued, "She was 19, Carly was 19! That meant she was going to make it through this surgery and everything else that she needs to go through to become 19. There was no reason to be afraid!"

Jim could start to see why this story needed to be heard. Fear can be converted into faith, but it is an inside job. Sandi finished the story with confidence. "I wiped off the mascara that was dripping down my eyes from crying, and composed myself. I walked back to the hospital noticing that people were staring at me along the way. What did I expect? I just ran by them screaming at the top of my lungs just minutes ago," she laughed to relive the tension from the recollection. Jim joined her. "When my husband saw me come back into the waiting room of the hospital, he asked me if I was okay. All I could say was, 'Carly is 19.'"

Jim stopped filming and leaned down towards Carly. "You're going to help a lot of people Miss Carly." She laughed. Jim took a photo with Carly and visualized the impact her piece would have in the film. In fact, he saw the premiere, he saw the audience and he saw the hit that this would be. "What a powerful message. If you can see it as done, you have no need to have any fear."

Chapter 23

PSYCHOLOGY OF REFERRALS
FLIP THE STATS

Three more weeks had gone by and Taz and Jim were filming away. They were able to put together a small clip of their film to show to prospects that were interested in helping them get it out. One person in particular saw promise in this film and decided to invest in the marketing aspect. Her name was Terri Simpson and she came onboard in an unusual way.

Jim and Taz decided it was time to take out a loan to help finance their plans with the film. They had extraordinary footage and stood back to honor their talent, along with others. Together they brought out the magic of these people and they hoped that these people would further see it in themselves. Just a week ago, Jim realized how big this could be, if they let their minds believe it. They created new visions as they grew and they focused on them daily.

"I made an appointment for us with a lender. I don't know how it's going to go, but it couldn't hurt. I've also made a marketing plan and where the money will go to bring attention to this film. I've taken the contacts we made along the way and I've included them in our vision movies. I've put them into the plan as resources for getting this movie out. And…. here's the other thing. We also have a theatre here who is going to do the screening and… they are sponsoring it." This was the first time Taz heard Jim sound calm and confident.

"How did you do all of this?" Taz asked.

"I threw myself in. I stayed up all of last night and remember Jessica with the film festival?" Jim said as he pulled up something on his laptop.

"Yeah," Taz answered.

"Well, she got us the theatre and she also volunteered all of her connections through the festival. In other words, all of these people…" he showed Taz the website of the festival on his computer. He scrolled down the list of names of the people involved in making it happen and the filmmakers, directors, actors and producers that would be there. She's going to send our film to them and ask them to promote us.

"You're incredible. What's gotten into you?" Taz asked.

"Well, not only the rush of all of these people, but I met with someone yesterday. Her name is Kathleen Nguyen and she really changed my perspective on ramping things up." Jim confessed.

"How so?" Taz asked.

Jim reflected back to his brief meeting with Kathleen who was a friend of the producer he was working for. He told her that he felt like he was just one connection away from making this whole thing happen. He needed a place to screen the film, he needed exposure and he needed some financial backing.

"I guarantee you know someone right now who can provide all of those things." She said with assurance.

"I guess. I just don't know who or how to ask."

"I built my entire career based on the psychology of referrals."

"What do you mean?" he asked.

"When I work with someone or meet with them, I give. I give them whatever I have to give. Sometimes, it's just knowledge and that makes them feel that they are taken care of. I happen to know one person in this building that can help you and based on what you've told me, you know her too. The question is will you ask for that help and what will you give?"

"So what did you tell her?" Taz asked.

"I told her I didn't know what to give!"

"So….?" Taz urged Jim to say more.

"She told me that what I have gone through in this journey and in my past was my gift to give others. She told me that my experience was useful to others. She said every person in this building and in my life has gone through something and that I should show them through my experience that no matter what you can get what you need and what you want."

"And obviously, you did."

"Jessica. I went back to her and I asked her what I could do for her. She told me that she wanted her message to be heard. In that moment, I took out my phone and let her speak. I don't think she ever felt safe to say what she wanted to say and as soon as we were done, she called a guy that owns a theater and here we are…" Taz was grateful and so was Jim. "The more we edit and the more I watch these people that we've connected with, Taz, the more I am filled with not only hope, but clarity. We are on this train man and it is moving with sheer momentum."

Two hours later, the guys were sitting down at a bank with a potential lender. She refused to let them film her, but her voice was still recorded. The camera was placed on the ground, where only feet were shown.

"I just think the odds are against you here. I'm sorry. Most people will view this as nothing more than a hobby. But, I do wish you well. Statistics on these things are just not working in your favor. There's just not enough for us to bank on here." The young woman sitting across from Taz and Jim closed the window on her computer and pushed herself away from her desk.

Taz and Jim looked at each other and took a moment before getting up.

Chapter 23

"Flip those stats." The woman sitting next to them said.

"What?" Taz responded.

"I heard her and I heard you. They are just stats and odds, that's all. Flip 'em and show them that you are in your favor."

"Who are you?" Jim asked.

"Terri Simpson. I'm finalizing a deal here and I overheard you. I hope that doesn't bother you. But, you were right next to me." Her voice was strong and she was instantly likeable.

Jim was intrigued. "Well I would love to flip those stats, I guess we just keep trying and looking?"

"Nah. I'll finance you."

Taz and Jim took a huge gulp. "What?" they said in unison.

"I've been wanting to invest in something that I believed in and I could really help you both. You put together a great marketing plan. Impressive."

"He did it one night!" Taz said.

"I got pregnant as a teen and I had ambition, but everyone told me that the odds were against me. When one woman told me that I would never amount to anything but a welfare mom, I made a promise to myself. I would not become my reality. I would not let anyone else determine my future but me. I don't buy into the stats and it's been the best decision I ever made. Just flip them and you will find what you are looking for." Terri said standing up.

"I think we just did." Taz said.

Chapter 24

GIVE AWAY TOO MUCH

The anticipation was reaching its all-time highest. After Terri invested with Taz and Jim, the ball was rolling faster than they could keep up with. They were filming along the way to capture as much as they can. They wouldn't be surprised if they added something in even at the last minute before the screening. The journey was that absorbing.

As the days were approaching and the screening was getting plugged in various venues, Jim realized that he wanted to give something. He remembered meeting Scott Carson along this path and suddenly his words were sounding louder in Jim's mind. He remembered the story of Scott's own rise and the hurdles he faced along the way.

"It's about closing the deal, not about making money."

"Isn't that the same thing?" Jim asked Scott during an afternoon conversation.

"Most people think it is. But, what is that deal to you? Is it just about making money? Because if it is, you probably won't see that person ever again. They were just a customer. Closing the deal in my book is about giving way too much."

"Giving way too much?" Jim asked.

"My parents always told me that I give away too much for what I charge. I always said, 'yeah and that's why they keep coming back.' When you give people more, you build a relationship that brings you more."

Jim found himself at the computer emailing Sandi. He remembered that she had a cause in the name of her daughter. He also found himself emailing Richard for the cause he supported. As he went through the rolodex of people that helped him make this film the moving piece that it was, he realized how much more he needed to give of this film. With each person, he asked where he could donate proceeds of this film. When Taz and Terri heard of this, they inserted it into the marketing materials so that everyone would feel more of a drive to see it and promote it.

After all of his emails were sent, he emailed Scott and simply said, "Thank you."

Chapter 25

AUTHENTICATION REQUEST

It was now days away from the screening of *The Rise*. Jim's nerves were through the roof. So many things still needed to be done. He wanted it to be perfect. Taz was hit with the flu and Jim was taking everything on. He needed help, but it was so hard to ask. He'd gotten good at accepting offerings, but to actually ask for it? That was hard. After a lethargic speech from Taz about asking for help without guilt, Jim finally called up a friend to come over.

Margaret Ziedin had just come back from being out of the country.

"You seem so beaten down right now, Jim." She said with her Australian accent and long wavy hair.

"I'm tired and I'm scared."

"This is a big moment approaching, I know. But, it is happening and you've got to be ready for it. People want to see that light in you."

"Ha! Light? I'm not feeling it right now. I keep thinking, what if it all goes wrong? What if they hate it? It'll be like college all over again."

"Hey hey!" Her voice was louder now. "From what I've seen, you two are magicians at capturing the light in others. The proof is on the screen. Maybe it's time you got proof of your own." She was firm.

"Ah. I don't know."

"Jim, that's what this is about." She walked over to the camera sitting on the kitchen counter. She knew just what she was doing. "Come over here."

"Why?"

"Stand right there." She directed him to stand in good lighting and she started the camera.

"What are you doing?"

"People want to see your light at the end of this, you know? This was ultimately your rise, wasn't it?" She asked. "You're rising right now. This is part of it, Jim. This is what they want to see. Inspire them."

She filmed him in that moment just standing there. He didn't know what to say.

"Make the choice, Jim." He still stood silent. "Or it will get made for you…" She almost sang.

A smile started to emerge on his face.

"Who are you Jim?" She waited. "Are you ready for this opportunity? Cause if you're not, it will go to someone else."

The seconds of silence felt like minutes.

Chapter 25

"I am Jim MacDonald and I am on my rise just like you."

Margaret smiled and put down the camera. She walked over and gave him a hug.

"I called you over to help with planning the event. I didn't know you were going to write the end."

She laughed. "Look at that footage later on and you will see who you are. This whole film is a reflection of you. It's something we all need. We need a reminder of who we are. So, whenever you feel this overwhelmed and doubtful, look at yourself in the mirror or better yet on film and give yourself the authentication request and affirm your light... know it's right."

Chapter 26

PUSH DON'T PULL

"Taz it's Jim, I need to talk to you ASAP," Jim left a message on Taz's voicemail.

Within minutes, Taz returned the call. "What's up?"

"I need to add another interview."

"What are you talking about? We don't have time. We have to get the final version over to them today." Taz was firm.

"I know but I got something so good and we need to put it in."

"There's no way we'll finish in time. Do you know how much stuff I need to get done in time for the premiere? Seriously, I just don't see how it's possible."

"Then I'll keep pushing," Jim said calmly.

"What are you talking about?" Taz asked.

"Go check your email, then call me back."

Just two hours before calling Taz, Jim ran into Kent Clothier while picking up extra microphones for the after show panel.

Jim was just getting off a frustrating call, when Kent, who walked in just behind him, "Trying to be everything?"

"Oh yeah, crazy day." Jim acknowledged. "How are you doing, Kent? Long time no see." Jim met Kent through Taz during one of their interviews.

"How's that film coming along?" Kent asked.

"It's coming. But, I'll tell you. There are some people that are supposed to be helping you that actually make the whole process a lot harder!" He laughed trying to make light of it and not seem melodramatic.

"Are you being true to your values?" Kent asked.

"Yeah, for the first time in my life I actually am." Jim said as if he just realized it

"Good, then you're pushing people away."

Jim paused and opened his mouth ready to respond, but not quite knowing what to say to that. "How's that? I was told you push people away when you aren't true to yourself."

"The reality is that you push people away by being real and clear because you are making a statement of who you are and what you trying to do."

"Wait, I'm confused. I don't want to push people away," Jim said immediately.

"Well, the way I see it. You do want to push people away and pull in the people that support your cause." He watched as Jim's perception started to change.

Chapter 26

"So, by being true to myself I pull in the right people and push away the wrong people." Jim nodded his head and then said, "It sounds easier actually."

"Look, people have a tendency to feel that they have to be everything to everybody. They worry that if they don't do everything, they will hurt those around them. Then they take on too much stuff that doesn't align with their core values. In falling into this pattern, they end up pushing away what they need and pulling in what they don't."

Jim looked at Kent and knew what he needed to do. "Um, is there anyway, you could repeat all of that again?" He paused for a moment. "On camera?"

Kent laughed out loud. "Sure, I could do that."

Chapter 27

THE LAST INTERVIEW

Taz got the last interview from Jim with Kent onto the final movie version and it was ready to be presented to the theater. Jim suggested to Taz that they need testimonials and quotes to validate the film's powerful messaging. In doing so, they connected with a friend of the theater who watched the film and was completely inspired. Time was short, so Jim and Taz agreed to record him and transcribe it later into something they could use.

"What is most important to you about rising?" Jim asked Yvan Gosselin well into the interview.

"Well, if the main objective remains to be the constant improvement of oneself ,then the desire to get better and grow makes the entire journey worth it," Yvan said with a French accent.

"Is that what motivates you?" Jim asked.

"What motivates me above all is to contribute to the success of others. In fact," he laughed, "it is why I am doing this for you. I believe in the messages of this film and I am deeply motivated by a great desire to learn more. This is why I am driven by my personal want to surpass myself and know excellence. I believe this film and all of the people in it have given me just that." Yvan smiled with great humbleness.

Jim and Taz looked at each other feeling complete fulfillment.

"This movie will make a real difference in people's lives because it not only provides wisdom, but it will remain in the consciousness of individuals. I have one request for you as it is my mission to help others succeed and I see that it is part of your mission as well."

"Of course," Taz and Jim said in unison.

"I would like to translate this into multiple languages around the world. If you will allow me to be a greater part of this, then nothing would make me happier than to influence others and bring them closer to their dreams."

Taz and Jim nearly fell to the floor when they heard was Yvan was offering. "Absolutely!" Jim exclaimed.

"We're in!" Taz said.

"Then let's go!" Yvan said.

Chapter 28

TOUCHING TORCHES

"And another torch is passed," Luba Rusyn was in the room with Taz and Jim helping them with the marketing for the premiere. She was a friend of Taz and his wife and she had great input as to how the film could be presented.

"Yeah?" Jim said. "How so?"

"Look at the raving testimonials you have," she replied. "You have a luminous torch. The film has the power to go on and on by lighting one torch after the other."

"I'm not sure I'm following you."

"Jim, with each interview you've done, you touched someone's torch."

"If you mean I've touched someone, I feel like they are the ones that have touched me!"

"Oh they have and that's the whole point!"

"What do you mean?"

"Your torch has been lit and by the multiple people you have aligned yourself with, your light has gotten brighter. By sharing this with the rest of the world, you are continuing to touch other torches and give them light as well."

Jim smiled at this. "I get it." He thought about it for another moment. "I really get it! Wow. I really like that. You know what started out as something to fill an empty place in me will actually fill many others.

"Keep doing it Jim. It doesn't have to stop here. You've got more in you. This I know." Luba smiled warmly.

Chapter 29

THE RISE

The day had come. Everything was in place and set in motion. There was a long line outside the theater. Jim and Taz, along with some technical crew were standing inside doing the last minute touches before the film would premiere.

"You guys ready?" The owner of the theater asked. "This is going to be huge."

Taz and Jim looked at each other and gave each other a long hug. Their moment had arrived and regardless how the documentary would be received, they had made it. They did it and they could only move up.

"Ready?" Taz prompted.

"Ready," Jim followed.

When the doors opened, the people came flooding in. They were talking a mile a minute. People who were in the film also filled the seats. Popcorn was already being spilled and laughs could already be heard. A brief introduction was made by Jessica, the crowd noise faded and the lights went out.

There were laughs. There were cries. There was shouting and there was cheering. And when the movie ended, there was silence for a moment on Jim's last words. But it didn't last long. As soon as the credits rolled, the applause was literally through the roof.

Jim's heart was filled with warmth. People rushed to hug him, including Taz' family. When the applause started to die down, Jim took the stage right in front of the screen.

"It's not an easy journey this ride they call life, but we are all on it. We are all on a rise. I want to thank each and every one of you for taking part in my rise and I hope you will continue yours as I will continue mine. I hope to see every one of your faces along the way and I can't wait to see you all at the top... wherever that may be..."

The cheering began again.

It was hours before the mayhem of adrenaline and enthusiasm died down. At the very end of the night after refreshments and conversations dwindled, one man came up to Jim. It was Charles, the man who refused to be part of the film.

"Congratulations," he said to Jim. He was much softer now than Jim remembered.

"Wow. You came." Jim acknowledged.

"Despite my rudeness, you still invited me."

Jim smiled.

"You know my daughter."

"I do?" Jim asked with confusion.

Chapter 29

He pointed his head to the front of the stage where Jessica stood.

"Jessica is your daughter?"

"My one and only, though she's not always proud of it," he laughed.

"I want to present something to you and I understand if you wish to decline," he was humbled.

"What's that?"

"The network is looking for something new and different and applicable to today's world. They'll back most anything I present to them and I'd like to pitch them the concept of a show called… The Rise," he paused for a moment. "Does that sound of interest to you?"

Jim held out his hand and smiled, "Mr. Miller? It's a deal I'd love to work with you."

The End

Co-Author Biographies

Aaron Young is the CEO of Laughlin Associates. His life's work has been to empower entrepreneurs to build strong businesses and then proactively protect what they have built. Aaron has consulted with business owners from around the world and built his own multi-million dollars companies. A published author and frequent guest on radio and television shows nationwide, Aaron has been an advocate for the small business owner for over 20 years. Aaron's goal is to arm entrepreneurs with formulas for success that can be applied immediately to create exponential growth and protection for their personal empire.

A leader in the business world, and an engaging speaker who speaks directly to the heart and mind of entrepreneurs, Aaron has consulted government leaders, participated on corporate boards of directors and mentored ultra-successful CEOs using six critical strategies that can make the difference between success and failure. Aaron can be reached at: 775-883-8484 or ayoung@laughlinusa.com.

Clarissa Burt is an award winning media personality, television producer, actress, emcee and top international supermodel with more than 25 years experience in the modeling and media industries. Her signature walk has been seen on most major runways in the world and she appeared on 250 magazine covers including Harpar's Bazaar, Vogue and Cosmopolitan to name a few. Clarissa was the worldwide face of Orlane Cosmetics, Carita's, Helena Rubenstein and Revlon campaigns. Her live television productions have included "The Miss Universe Pageant Italy" and "Backstage with The Miss for Miss Universe." Clarissa has performed in over 20 movies. A leading authority on beauty, image, and self-esteem, "Good Morning, Italy" called upon Clarissa to host the popular beauty segment, "Clarissa Suggests." She hosted her own radio show entitled "Clarissa Burt Talks" on voice America and world talk radio interviewing renowned entrepreneurs and thought leaders. Runway Beauty magazine brought Clarissa on board as Health and Beauty Editor for their 2008 launch. She is currently launching The International Model University and The Clarissa International Model Search and Awards. Clarissa has recently launched the International Model University and The International Model Search and Awards. Her weekend intensive workshop is the perfect hands on course designed to give participants an idea of what it is like working in the modeling and fashion industries. Also a Director, Scout, Instructor, and Resource for the International Model and Talent Association (IMTA), Clarissa hand-picks and develops talent showcasing them in front of 300 agents from all over the world. Ms. Burt's Book "The Self-Esteem Regime" is due for Fall 2012 distribution. Clarissa's mission is and always will be the betterment of women. You can find more on Clarissa at www.ClarissaBurt.com.

Deborah Ives Lillywhite is a wife, mother of 11 and grandmother of 13. She has been an entrepreneur for over 20 years and has built several multi million dollar businesses from the ground up. She is an award-winning speaker and has the distinction of being a Master at manifesting. She has been called the "Queen of short sales" way before the industry knew what a short sale was. As co owner of the Orange County Investors Club, she has the opportunity to be a teacher and mentor to many real estate investors all over the country. Deborah is also a contributing author to the national best seller "Initiative" with Greg Reid. You can reach Deborah through www.expertforeclosurerelief.com, Deborah.lillywhite@gmail.com or by phone, 714-900-5708.

Flor Mazeda is a highly motivated entrepreneur with extensive experience in management skills who currently owns and operates a retail business through a large processing facility. Originally from Mexico, Flor moved to the United States in 1989. Following a string of unsuccessful business endeavors she, along with her husband Fidel, started a small Real Estate Investment company in 1998. In 2002 she started her business, a cafeteria that caters to over 800 employees at a large processing plant. After seeing the need for a new approach to educational tools, Flor developed "My Way to College System", an organizational system and training program based on the premise of taking each child's own achievements and use them as steppingstones to build their future career in College, University or Technical School. Flor's love for education shows by having graduated twice from High School, once in Mexico in 1988 and in 1992 in the USA, the same year she would have received her degree as a Chemical Engineer from UANL. Flor lives in Texas with husband Fidel, daughters Kimberly, Katty and Stephanie and two grandkids. You can reach Flor at flor.mazeda@gmail.com.

Forrest May entered this world as the son of a farmer and a school teacher. His childhood was spent in Kansas on the farm in the summer and in the southwestern US where his mother taught during the school year. In high school, his question for what career to pursue was very limited. Farm folk are some of the nicest people you will ever meet, but their understanding of job opportunities are all farm related. As a result, he ended up blending a teaching career with a major in earth science and mathematics. His first high school teaching job in Yuma, Arizona, kept him occupied for the next 23 years. It was there where he worked on helping students see the future and plan a life that they were in charge of. His desire to help others led to a prison detention center ministry based on self-worth and self-responsibility. During the years of teaching, Forrest had the time to purchase rental houses, learn the fix up trade, and become a landlord. He is proudest of the renters who he encouraged to save up money and purchase their own home. He sincerely feels that we all have a past; may we remember the good parts only. We all have a future; it will get here soon enough. We live in the present and allow our thoughts to lead us into opportunities that create our future. He continues to encourage people to live their dreams not someone else's dream. He lives with his life and business partner, Deborah Clark in Yuma, Arizona. Forrest can be reached at maytradingpost@gmail.com.

Greg Ausley is the founder of LifeSpace.com. LifeSpace helps people set, track and achieve goals in all areas of life, both professionally and personally. Prior to LifeSpace, Ausley co-founded and ran REApplications until it was acquired in 2008 and used his newly found freedom to embark on an ambitious project to help the world get excited about achieving their biggest dreams in life. He has assisted tens of thousands of individuals with their goals and is now working on altering the way corporations inspire their professionals.

He is a serial goal-setter and in his spare time, runs marathons, invests in real estate, travels and contributes back to the world by helping raise the bar on the foster system. To contact Greg, please visit LifeSpace.com/GregAusley or email gausley@lifespace.com.

Jake Ducey is a twenty-year-old author, speaker/seminar leader, activist, and poet who has devoted himself to reconstructing our world by the power of three: Passion-Power-Purpose. Since 2012 Jake has traveled to Guatemala, Australia, Indonesia, and Thailand. In 2011 he raised funds to build a school in San Marcos, near Lake Atitlan in Guatemala. He also raised the funds for a home to accommodate orphans who are taken care of by a Quiché Maya Shaman in San Marcos. Since beginning his odyssey of world travels, including discoveries with the Maya,

Australian entrepreneurs, and Thai Monks, he has come to work with Timeless Learning Center, Youth Wellness Network, and author two books. His works include: Into the Wind; My Six-Month Journey Wandering the World for Life's Purpose (Release: TBD) Jake can be reached at jake@jakeducey.com.

Jonathan C. Carter Businesses looking for transformation of products or processes, looking for a blissful relationship between function and cost, seek Jonny's systematic approach. He is an expert in the process of designing solutions in the form of product designs, production systems, or efficient business processes. There are many hidden barriers to creating or transforming a system that most people are completely unaware of that Jonny addresses. His approach takes whats truly important in the situation, designs a system solution targeted on specific needs, and transforms bland performance into that which is desired in any business situation. You can find more about Jonny at www.JonathanCCarter.com.

Joshua S. Phair is a sought after systems creator, independent trainer, author and speaker. He started three companies at age 21 in a foreign country and language. He experienced massive growth and has dedicated the last 12 years to teaching others how to reach their goals. His curiosity caused him to research network marketing compensation plans extensively and in the capacity of consultant; he has created four compensation plans for network marketing companies; he has mentored three companies over and around the hurdles and obstacles that cause failure in their first year; and he has helped with innovative solutions on the duplication side of the networking industry. He has touched the lives of thousands across two continents and currently resides in Utah with his Wife and five children. He can be reached at joshuaphair@gmail.com.

Kathleen Nguyen is a Real Estate Broker for Lifetime Real Estate, Inc. A real estate brokerage firm that she founded in 2004 located in Poway California. Kathleen's business philosophy is to treat others as she would like to be treated. The company's mission is provide the best customer service that can possibly be provided with the resources and skills that are available. Kathleen's clients are some of the happiest and most knowledgeable home buyers and sellers in San Diego today. That's because her first priority when meeting a new client is to find out how she can best help them. She actively listens and gives them the information they need to move through the process of buying or selling a home with the least possible stress or uncertainty. Kathleen's belief is that knowledge of today's market leads to good decisions. When clients know what to expect at each step along the way, it makes the entire transaction more enjoyable for everyone. A true "people person," Kathleen's respects the fact that this isn't like any other purchase – unless you're an investor, your home is where you live and raise your family. Her sense of empathy for the emotion that goes into buying or selling a home could be the reason why so many of her former clients are her present friends. A San Diego native, Kathleen gives back to her community and is on the board of AREAA (Asian Real Estate Associaion of America) to help facilitate home ownership among the Asians in San Diego County. Kathleen is also a member of Nahrep, SDAR, CAR and NAR. She can be reached at www.Lifetime-RE.com, Kathleen@Lifetime-RE.com or 858-842-1805.

Kent Clothier is the President and CEO of the REI Marketing, LLC, a multi-faceted real estate education and marketing company based in Boca Raton, FL. Under the REI umbrella, Kent owns and operates three multi-million dollar a year marketing brands including 1-800-SELL-NOW, Find Cash Buyers NOW and Find Private Lenders NOW; each of which is designed to help real estate investors and agents reach a specific marketing niche. Mr. Clothier also owns and operates MemphisInvest, one of the largest real estate investment companies in the country. Kent has experience early success at the age of 23, taking over organizations and growing annual revenue to over $80 million. After various more experiences, his investing career was born. A founding member of the over 350 member Mid-South REIA, the Clothier family's proven track record in real estate is staggering. He's introduces many revolutionary products such as FindCashBuyersNOW.com, which solved the long-standing problem of investors finding buyers for their homes. Lastly in 2010, Kent solved another long standing challenge for real estate professionals, finding private lenders in their area to provide creative financing for their transactions. Kent and his wife Seema, have been married since 2003, and have two wonderful children. Kent is one of the country's most sought after speakers and pours a great deal of his energy into helping normal people to unlock their true potential in their business and personal development. To learn more, visit: www.KentClothier.com.

Lori Taylor says that the best way to have a massive impact on the world doesn't come from playing it safe. Too many people today hedge their bets with plan B's, C's and even D's. It gets so convoluted at times you forget what plan A even was. Playing to win means you keep your eye on the ball and you swing for the fences. And while winning might not be everything, she believes wanting to is! Only you set the limits of what you can do! Unshackling her soul from the corporate world with a leap of faith in 2009, she started her own agency REV Media Marketing, LLC coining the phrase given to her by her young son, "You bring the rain, we'll make it pour." She learned to run her own race from her heart, with the mantra, "say what you do and do what you say, and always show people you care." Everything she does is fueled by these beliefs. From angel investing in disruptive startups (like Klout) to motivational speaking to marketing consulting, she always wants to challenge herself, her friends and her clients to "run your own race"; cautioning you to never change who you are. Social CaffeineT is the platform she's created to bring these beliefs to life - to your brand. Lori R Taylor believes in emboldening others to give voice and energy to their game-changing ideas. This commitment to always playing by her heart is probably why she made the list at as a top 50 Social Media Power Influencer.

In fact, in 2011 Mari Smith, the pied piper of Facebook according to Fast Company, listed Lori as a Top 10 Social

Media Super. Lori was also recently named to the board of the prestigious California's Women's Conference, the largest women's conference in the world. With past speakers such as Oprah, Michelle Obama, Katie Couric and Diane Sawyer, Lori is looking forward to being a featured speaker at the event in September 2012. Lori has graced the stage with world renowned motivational speakers Les Brown, John Assaraf, Greg Reid, Gary Goldstein, Rhonda Britten, and Mari Smith. Lori cherishes these opportunities to inspire new and amazing audiences with her beliefs and teachings, showcasing her talent for easily connecting with any audience.

To connect with Lori you can find her at:
Her blog http://lorirtaylor.com
Twitter http://twitter.com/lorirtaylor
Facebook http://facebook.com/loriraylene
LinkedIn http://linkedin.com/in/lorirtaylor

Luba S. Rusyn is a business promoter. She is a diverse industry entrepreneurial success. In 1993 she supplemented her business wisdom with formal knowledge by earning a Bachelor of Commerce degree. Her success can be attributed to her ability to translate this combination of knowledge and wisdom into efficient and effective results. Her enchantment with business spans 30 years, from the family farm, where she became skilled at production and bartering product price with wholesalers (Sunkist) to large organizations such as the Edmonton Oilers Hockey Club (1984-85 Stanley Cup) and Meyers Norris Penny LLP (public accounting). As a business owner/operator (elk ranching, Laundromats, dental offices, coaching/consulting), Luba understands entrepreneurial challenges and thus provides her clients with objective and actionable advice that promotes their success. You can reach Luba at luba@rsp360.com.

Business mentor and trusted friend, **Margaret Ziedin** is a GM for a retail development project on The Strip in Las Vegas, NV. Originally from Sydney, Australia she is an accomplished international entrepreneur. Margaret's formula for success teaches and inspires others to courageously embrace their true life purpose. Her bold and globally resourceful style attracts masterminds in the making, who she likes to partner with in business ventures.

Margaret competes in 5150s & Ironman 70.3s, she finished Silverman known as the "World's Toughest Triathlon" her true prize being the 3rd greatest fundraiser for Challenged Athletes Foundation's® (CAF). She continues to race for a reason by dedicating all her races to CAF who assists challenged athletes by bridging the financial gap and overcome funding obstacles blocking their path to athletic achievement by the provision of prosthetic equipment, special coaching and the like. The gift of sports helps get challenged athletes off the sidelines, and into the game...it changes lives in the most positive way.

Margaret believes motivation and passion become most rewarding when we give all of ourselves to the benefit others. Connect with Margaret at twitter: @hippyfairy or margaret@ziedin.com.

Born and bred New Yorker, former executive trailblazer, **Maria Gamb** spent more than twenty years in the trenches of corporate America directing and managing successful businesses valued in excess of $100 million. Companies she worked for in various capacities included Macy's, Geoffrey Beene, Liz Claiborne, and Polo-Ralph Lauren in roles such as Designer, Product Manager and Director. Maria has also lived in both England and Australia as well as working extensively internationally.

Maria brings her 20 plus years of global experience to others helping corporate leaders and entrepreneurs reclaim their ability to lead dynamic businesses steeped in values, communication, collaboration and teamwork. She has been called the "Rubik's Cube" of business due to her unique ability to breakdown problems, roadblocks and challenges into the smallest pieces, then reassemble those businesses and leadership into a fully functioning form.

Maria Gamb is known for her straightforward, honest and often humorous approach to building business relationship and leadership that gets results. She is a champion of women, business and value-based leadership as a sought after consultant to entrepreneurial and executive women.

She is a monthly contributor at Forbes magazine and co-hosts a national radio show. She speaks internationally, hosts numerous workshops and the powerhouse "Value to Vision Retreat" throughout the year. Her first book "Healing The Corporate World" quickly became an Amazon Top 10 Best Seller in the category of business leadership within hours of release. She has also been a contributor on 3 additional books. She can be reach www.MariaGamb.com and www.HealingTheCorporateWorld.com. She can also be followed by twitter @mariagamb.

Miranda Larson is an experienced JV Manager for several exclusive clients including John Assaraf, Doug Bench, Scotty Saks, The Expert Radio Network and broker for many more. Her focus is business relationships, creative business development, and many different types of events that speakers, authors, internet marketers, information marketers and entrepreneurs find necessary to make their businesses successful in today's market. She has developed a JV Matrix that includes several different mastermind groups and coordinates JV's in an array of business genres. Miranda brings a wealth of knowledge of networking techniques, collaboration and building business relationships skills. Training Networking leaders and member organizations to get the most out of their networking experiences has been a passion. Her goal is to help business owners improve their networking skills, and build solid relationships that will ultimately boost their bottom line. Last year, the participants in one of her high level masterminds generated over 2 million dollars in sales through collaborations in a six month period of time. Miranda's diverse business experience encompasses being on the board of directors for a tax preparation company as well as served on the board of directors for several networking organizations: AMG, Referral Exchange Network, Network Your Life, and 4U Network. She has planned and executed company launches, product launches and a variety of other events, as well as run a small catering company. And last but not least, she is the Chief Executive Mom of emomrewards.com. Miranda can be reached at larson.miranda@gmail.com.

Misha Elias was born and raised in Mexico City, Mexico. He came to the United States in 1990 when he was 20 years old. As many immigrants, he came to the country looking not for a guarantee of success, but for a chance to succeed. Being an illegal immigrant, he couldn't register for school so he learned to speak, read and write the English language on his own. He worked through several mediocre jobs until in 1994 when he found a job at a car dealership. He started as a sales person and became a Finance Manager after just nine months. He held that position for 13 years, making over six figures a year. While the money was good, he realized he had no time to spend with his family. He learned that if he wanted to gain free time and increase his financial position, he would need to go into business for himself. He also learned that in order to achieve dreams, you need determination, discipline, commitment and guidance from other successful people in order to create success. Misha understands that there are many ups and downs in life, same as in business, and that as long as he keeps committed to his goals he can rise up again when faced with challenges. Misha became a US Citizen in 2002 and is now a successful Real Estate Investor and Entrepreneur. He coaches and helps people to find the same opportunity to succeed in their lives. You can reach Misha at 562-688-5886 or by email at michael.elias@gmail.com.

Natalie Ledwell is a Law of Attraction evangelist. She positively impacts the lives of thousands of people around the world every day by empowering them to achieve their dreams by first knowing what they want then creating a personal "digital" vision board or Mind Movie to invoke the principles of The Law of Attraction. She grew up in Orange NSW Australia number 5 in a family of eight children. At the age of 18 she left her family, friends and everything she knew and moved to Sydney to pursue a career in Fitness. It was at the age of 21 she realized it was possible to achieve anything she set her mind to when was introduced to Personal Development motivational information in the form of a set of Brian Tracey cassette's her boss lent to her. In 1995 she met her husband Glen and they embarked on a 10 year serial entrepreneurship owning and operating a long list of businesses. Years of seminars, books, goal setting, weekend retreats, hot coal walking combined with hard work and just about every type of business under the sun, left her feeling frustrated, helpless and questioning what else could she do to live the life she always dreamed of. In 2006 Natalie experienced a life changing epiphany when she watched a movie called The Secret. This lead her down an inspired path of Law of Attraction research and application. Now Natalie gratefully lives a life beyond her wildest dreams. She lives an endless summer, travels the world, and has an incredible circle of friend who share her positive mindset and provides amazing support. She calls her mentors Bob Proctor, John Assaraf, Bob Doyle and Joe Vitale, friends. She wakes up next to her perfect partner, sees the ocean from her apartment, drives a beautiful car that she didn't think she could ever afford, eats out when she wants and doesn't check the price tag on the clothes she buys. In 4 short years Natalie along with her husband Glen and business partner Ryan Higgins built a multimillion dollar online business and are grateful that through this business they are making a difference. Natalie is currently writing a book to further reach more people and spread the Law of Attraction message. She is also sharing her practical, entertaining and poignant journey on stage to any audience willing to have her. Her favorite food is a toss-up between sushi and cheese and her favorite pastime is great food, great wine, great conversation with great friends all around the world. Natalie can be reached at natalie@mindmovies.com.

In 1977, at the age of twenty **Richard Barrier** read Think and Grow Rich. In 1978, he started his corporate career working with large computer systems. Since then he has been laid off twice in 1993 and in 2003, just four days before leaving for Peru. A dream he had since he was twenty, Richard went anyway. In June 2009, Richard started his first business. Six weeks later he was told that the department was being shutdown and that his last day was September 30th. On September 10th he received an e-mail about a

Think and Grow Rich: Three Feet From Gold event just five miles from where he lived. Richard did not know any of the speakers but that October event changed his life. On January 2011, Richard started his second business. He took his specialized knowledge of computer languages and applied it to smartphones, he hired himself. Over the Top Projects LLC is a software development company focused on parental controls of smartphones. In April 2012, with the encouragement of his mastermind group, Over the Top Projects LLC's first smartphone app was released. It is called TXT ME L8R, it prevents Distracted Driving from texting. There are 5,500 deaths per year with one and a half million accidents per year from Distracted Driving. Richard can be reached at richard@overthetopprojects.com or at 1-88TXTMEL8R.

Richard J. Muscio is a CPA with 30 + years of experience, whose technical specialty is estate/gift/trust matters. Known as "The Family Office Guy," Richard serves "of counsel" to 6 Family Offices, where he assists the "in-house" CPA/CFO. Richard helps wealthy families to reduce estate taxes, understand their complex financial situations, and communicate more effectively. Richard is Founder of the Move Your Feet Before You Eat Foundation, as well as the Oceanside Turkey Trot and the Vista Strawberry Fest 5k. His Foundation focuses on improving public school student physical fitness, replacing junk food snack options with healthy food choices, and reducing teen pregnancy in the Oceanside and Vista public school systems. More information can be found at www.osideturkeytrot.com. If you think you had a lot of people over for Thanksgiving, well Richard hosted 12,000, and he ran the 5k through downtown Oceanside in a turkey costume. Richard arranges monthly speakers for San Diego's most prestigious collaboration platform STAR-San Diego, website www.star-sandiego.com. He also hosts a weekly radio show on 760 AM KFMB on Sunday evenings from 7-8 PM, please go to www.iymoney.com if you want to see his caricature as he has a face made for radio. He can be reached at: rjm@fabcpas.com.

Growing up in the Cleveland area, **Rick Gresh** knew he wanted to be a chef at age 12. He earned his associate degree in culinary arts at the nationally renowned Culinary Institute of America. While in school, he landed an impressive externship at the Waldorf Astoria in New York City and after graduation went on to work at many acclaimed Chicago restaurants including Trio, Celebrity Café at the Nikko Hotel, and Tsunami. At just 23, Rick accepted the executive chef position at Chicago's hip jazz club, Green Dolphin Street. The restaurant thrived under his leadership and won a three-star review from the Chicago Tribune. He moved on to such prestigious restaurants as the award-winning Caliterra Restaurant at the Wyndham

Hotel Chicago and the Saddle & Cycle Club. In 2001 Rick Gresh was invited to host his first dinner at the James Beard House & was named a "Rising Star of American Cuisine." In 2004 and 2006 he was a USA competition finalist in the world's premier culinary competition, the Bocuse D'Or.

A modern steakhouse menu is featured at David Burke's Primehouse, where Rick Gresh is currently the Executive Chef. During the last two years, Rick has earned AOL best fine dining restaurant in Chicago, Chicago Reader best steakhouse, Chicago Magazine best dry-aged steak & best bread, and Gayot top-ten steakhouses in America. Most recently he has been named one of five "men to watch" by Chicago Magazine as well as Chef Humanitarian of the Year 2011 by Plate Magazine. Currently Rick is the host of the Watch312.com Internet show, "Chef City." Chef Gresh is known for his innovation in the culinary world. In 2012, after two years of research and development, he co-launched a brand-new cut of beef, the Vegas Strip Steak. He also recently developed a way to produce barrel-aged meats and cheeses using spent bourbon barrels. Currently he is writing his first cookbook, the first of its kind ever to be written. For updates on his projects, check out www.rickgresh.com. He can be reached at rg@rickgresh.com.

Sandi Gugliotti is a business owner and a mom. While combining the two is sometimes challenging, the love for her children continues to be the driving force in her life and in her business. She has spent many years working with Real Estate Professionals, Investors, and Bankers, by providing education and networking opportunities in a Seminar Environment. She is quoted saying, "I love the work that I do, and have met the most amazing people during my career. I have really found my passion." She can be reached at sandi.shaner@gmail.com.

Savannah Ross is the President of Rich Mom Enterprises Inc, an education based company dedicated to teaching a down to earth approach on creating great wealth through real estate investing. After a dramatic series of tragic events Savannah found herself on the brink of bankruptcy. Without any previous investment knowledge she then created over $3.1 Million in just 6 months. Just two years later, Savannah became the largest individual buyer of Real Estate in the Nation for 2009. Her system teaches a simple formula to acquiring high equity, high cash flow properties. Savannah will be the first to tell you that she is not passionate about real estate or wealth. She has found them to be effective tools to allow her to follow her true passion of helping those less fortunate. By helping others create ultimate freedom, they too can follow their true purpose. She is dedicated to empowering others to create their own success stories.

Savannah and her family enjoy giving back by building homes and feeding families in third world countries. Find more information at www.richmom.com.

Scott Carson grew up in South Texas in a small town called Ingleside. A four-sport letter in high school, he was the only student to land a full ride via academic and athletic scholarships via my success on the football field. He was the first of his dad's 10 kids to complete and graduate from college with a degree in business from Southwest Texas State University in San Marcos Texas in 2001. After college, he found his niche in the finance industry as a financial advisor and mortgage banker. After working in the banking industry, he started investing in real estate part time and made the full time jump when he helped create a mortgage company aligned with a real estate investment education and note buying company. After a short stint (6 months) of successful deals, he was recruited to start teaching new investors how to get started. After investing and training other investors for two years, he created Inverse Investments, LLC, my own real estate investment firm focused on buying defaulted mortgage direct from banks. He's now an international speaker featured at the National Association of Realtors conference, National Real Estate Investors Association, along with being quoted in the Wall Street Journal and Investor's Business Daily. He enjoys travel, music, reading, writing, boating, golf, and sports. He calls Austin, TX home but you will often find him splitting his time between San Diego and South Florida. His website is www.weclosenotes.com and he can be contacted at scott@weclosenotes.com or via phone at 512-585-3810.

Until recently, **Sonja Sbitani** was puzzled why her life took her to a foreign land away from her home in Germany at the age of 16, with just a few words of English to lean on. During the past 30 years of living in the United States, she learned to embrace the world's cultural differences through her career in Aviation and has gained valuable experience as a successful entrepreneur. The joys of being blessed with a family, learning to love unconditionally, enduring the painful loss of loved ones, struggling with her personal health challenges, and holding someone in her arms fighting for their last breath, brought her to the conclusion that life's distractions have blurred its true meaning of harmony and authenticity. Her frustration with life's distractions along with her desire to find solutions pushed her to find truth and what deeply lies in her heart: being part of helping people live better lives. She has now dedicated her life's work to touching many lives through the creation of her Quantum Living Foundation.

Concepts and Designs were formed, and her vision of Eco Wellness™ Centers and Villages was born. With her love and passion for people and our land and a clear focus on bringing people together to share resources and vital solutions to our modern day problems while embracing an eco-friendly and sustainable lifestyle, her desire to unite the world one community at a time is no longer just a concept. Through her collaborative partnership with a global infrastructure and development firm, she is bringing dynamic and diverse cultures together by serving their Wellness, Educational, Vocational, and Cultural needs, built on a foundation of integrity and transparency.

Eco Wellness™ Centers and Villages are being built nationally and globally through private funding. To become part of the solution or inquire about building a center in your community, contact Sonja@QuantumLivingGroup.com.

Tara Henson is a successful sales, marketing and operations executive who is driven by challenges. She has over 13 years of achievements in sales, marketing, and operations leadership, driving business and revenue growth in Fortune 500 companies and start-ups. Tara has over 12 years of experience in media ranging from Television, Out-of-Home and Digital. She began her media career in San Francisco, California during the Dot Com era. In 2007 she left the comfortable career in television for Hearst Argyle to start her own business. In 2009, she co-founded Initiative G, an environmental marketing firm. As VP of

Sales and Marketing for Initiative G, she consulted with Fortune 500 companies on their environmental initiatives and developed strategies to execute their outreach campaigns. She is a member of the Alliance for Women in Media Foundation, AWRT and is a committee chair for the Sacramento Children's Home. You can reach Tara at tarahenson@yahoo.com.

Terri Simpson is a senior level executive with 25 years combined experience in media, digital, out of home, sales, advertising and marketing. She is greatly experienced with start-ups to Fortune 500 companies. She is entrepreneurial in nature with the unique ability to build highly effective teams to execute aggressive goals. She has excellent communication skills with a tremendous ability to build positive relationships with clients and vendors. She is an effective manager of projects, operations, sales, marketing and advertising and a strategic thinker. She has the ability to understand client's underlying business and organizational issues. Terri is the founder of two successful start-ups, Radio Active Networks and CityReach Latino, operating in the top 11 Hispanic Markets. She can be reached at terrisimpson@inititiativeg.com.

From an early age, **Yvan-Serge Gosselin**, PhD. was destined for the uncommon professional achievement. He climbed the ladder of success by adopting a very positive attitude, finding confidence and enthusiasm to be the essential tools of a future winner. Through hard lessons engendered in adversity, he has also learned to take the necessary distance in order to rebound when faced with the seemingly insurmountable. Holding a Ph.D. from the University of Montreal, the co-author has taught for 20 years at universities in Canada, displaying a fundamental desire for constant learning, and sharing that learning with his students in such a way as to instill in them a taste for success derived from principles of constant self improvement. He now devotes a second career to business, bringing his wealth of experience to bear in advising and counseling captains of industry with winning strategies. Having completed a world tour, during which he had the immense opportunity to meet business people of many different cultures, he is focusing his current efforts on writing books about success and wealth. With the knowledge and varied experience he has garnered over the years, he gives generously of his time to advise people on finding the path to success and enthusiasm in their daily lives. He is in this respect a strong advocate of the principles of success taught by illustrious authors such as Dr. Napoleon Hill and Dr. Norman Vincent Peale. He can be reached at sergei11@videotron.ca.

Want More Life Nuggets? Here Are a Few From Sherpa Press

Everything is Subject to Change:
Finding Success When Life Shifts

Realizing that in both life and business, everything is subject to change. A super-successful businesswoman takes on an unlikely protege and teaches her how to adjust - and thrive - in an ever-evolving society and new economic reality. Almost before you realize it, the student, and single-working Mom, applies the wisdom she has learned and transforms her life in a remarkable way. Throughout this fast-paced business allegory, you will be encouraged and motivated to believe in your dreams, while being equipped with practical insights for transforming them into existence.

Off the Coast of Zanzibar:
Coming of Age for a Second Time

An adventurous tale that will inspire your soul and awaken your heart. Meet Karl, an entrepreneur and family man with an adventurous streak, who just realized success after years of learning through trial and error. Greeting you at the foot of Mount Kilimanjaro, he's accompanied by life's greatest nemesis: anxiety and fear. As he works out his trepidation along the ever-changing terrain of the mountain, his mind shifts from his past experiences to his present journey. Along the trek, he finds answers to the questions of how he got there and more importantly seeks where he will go next. This swift, page-turning parable is filled with metaphors and symbolic inspiration which will challenge you to believe that our dreams are realities just waiting for us to get there.

Initiative:
Looking beyond the Job and Into Lasting Achievement

Morgan Kingsbury just got laid off her dreary job. The search for her next gig leads her to a serendipitous meeting with someone who urges her to look beyond getting into another cubicle and into her sense of fulfillment in life. As she moves forward in her journey, she discovers what others did to find the initiative that led them towards continuous achievement. Following Morgan through chance encounters, she realizes her biggest dream. She also comes across the challenges that go alongside reaching her dream. You'll fall in love with Morgan in this animated, easy to read parable packed with laughs and inspirations of perseverance. She proves every dream is just initiatives away from reality.

Have a story to share?
Be featured in one of our best-selling titles.

Email **Allyn@sherpapress.com** today and learn how to participate in an upcoming collaboration.

You can also visit us at: **www.sherpapress.com**